The Scrapbook

A Novel

Jody Preister

Prelude

Jody Preister and husband, Bob, live just outside
Humphrey, Nebraska where they enjoy the many pleasures
of a simple life. When not writing, she enjoys spending
time with their grandchildren, helping out at their church,
or dabbling in the visual arts. Her most pleasurable activity
is riding with Bob on his Harley Davidson motorcycle. This
second novel was inspired from a short journal discovered
after her mother's death. Her mother's handwritten notes
recorded a time during the depression when she and her
two sisters traveled with their mother to California working
odd jobs and performing as acrobats and contortionists. The
four women lived and worked in the Los Angeles' area for
approximately eight months before returning to Nebraska.
With her mother's notes and a vivid imagination Jody has
woven together a series of events leading to a tender and
captivating love story which leaves the reader pondering
that perhaps there really are no coincidences in life.
Although some of the events presented in *The Scrapbook*
might be based on real life experiences, only those who
know the family history very well will be able to unravel
the possible truth from the purely fictional.

The following are a sampling of customer reviews of "The
Scrapbook" posted during the 2008 Amazon Breakthrough
Novel Award Contest:

"It put tears in my eyes and a lump in my throat and a
sweet melody in my heart."

"This would make a great Lifetime movie!"

"Jody's first book, *Third & Grace* was very interesting and
I have read and re-read it several times. I know this one
will be as good or better!"

"The writer has an expressive way of using words to describe the feelings and events of the storyline enabling you to vividly visualize the scene as if you were watching it on screen!"

"This story really touched me. It's an important story, the kind that matters in the grand scheme of things."

Dedication

The idea for this book came from my dear friend, Vicki Tanner. She shared the story of how she and her mother purchased an old scrapbook from an antique store and enjoyed reading about the life of a woman from the early twentieth century. Thank you, Vicki, for providing the idea for this story and especially for your friendship.

The inspiration for this book came from notes I found of my mother's after her death in September of 2003. She wrote about a time when she and her siblings left with their mother and went to California during the late nineteen-thirties. There are many similarities between Momma's notes and the stories in *The Scrapbook,* but only those who knew her very well will know what could be truth and what is purely fictional. Thank you, Momma, for all the love you gave and especially for the memories you left behind for us to pass on.

The support for this book came from my family and friends and especially from my dear husband, Bob. He is the love of my life and is so tolerant of the mess I make at our desk in the home office while I write. Thank you for supporting me and giving me the freedom to be creative and especially for loving me as I am.

The strength for this book (and everything I do) is given to me from God through faith in his son, Jesus and the power of the Holy Spirit. Without Him in my life, I am nothing. All that I do...all that I am...is because of what I believe. Thank you, Lord for my many blessings and the grace you provide for me daily but especially for loving me...in spite of who I am or what I've done.

1.

She placed the old, worn scrapbook on the counter as the clerk turned it over and removed the small price tag taped to its back. The cover was smooth leather, tan in color; bound with a red cord woven though two holes on each cover side and tied with a bow on the front. Inside were the memories of another life. A life that Glenda Ashbury was certain would be more stimulating than that of her own.

"Five dollars, please," the clerk stated dryly, slipping the scrapbook into a plastic grocery bag, probably donated by another customer. She was totally oblivious to the precious remnants of another life that just left her hands.

Glenda leaned against the wooden diamond willow cane and reached in her front jean pocket pulling out a crumpled five dollar bill and handing it to the clerk, saying, "Thanks." Quickly she lifted bag containing her discovery from the counter and exited the store; balancing her gait with the help of her cane. Her heart raced as she anticipated getting the scrapbook home and really looking through its pages. While at the thrift store she had glanced through it briefly, but didn't want to draw attention to the pages and their contents. There was something very special about this scrapbook and she wanted to explore it for herself in the privacy of her own home.

"Hey, Prince Snarls!" Glenda carefully reached down to stroke the large, gray, striped cat that greeted her as she walked through the door. He purred responsively at the touch of her hand. "Look what I found." She placed the bag on the old wooden trunk, used for a coffee table, in the living room and carefully removed the scrapbook. Prince Snarls jumped up on the trunk and curiously sniffed the bag and the scrapbook. "No, it's not for you. It's for me...a treasure I found at the thrift store. But we'll slowly look through it together, okay?" With that, the large cat jumped from the table to the sofa where Glenda was sitting. He leaped up the back and rested on the patch work quilt placed across the top where he began grooming himself; disinterested in any treasure his mistress thought she had acquired.

Glenda took her cane and went to the kitchen to get some ice from the freezer. She plopped the cubes into a glass, and then filled the glass with raspberry tea. "It's so hot outside; Snarly…you can be glad you are a house cat!" She said, plopping a partial ice cube into the water dish on the floor. The cat paused and looked but resumed his grooming as Glenda sat down on the sofa facing her treasure and carefully opened the front cover. On the first page was this hand written message:

My mom, my sisters and I left for California. Daddy had to stay behind and try to keep the business going. He makes shoes, but no one is buying shoes right now because there isn't any work and no money. We are going to California to try and earn some money. It was hard to leave.

Directly across from the message, on the following page, pressed between two yellowed pieces of cotton cloth, were a dried and faded little rose and another note that read:

Don't lose your way. Find your trellis, Betty Ann. Love, Dad

******

Five hundred miles away, at the Briarwood Hills Nursing Home, Betty Ann Bryant sits in a wheel chair gazing out the window of her room at the climbing rose bush sprawled out across a broken trellis. The days are long and monotonous for her now; a victim of old age and a recent stroke which has inhibited her outward beauty, mobility and desire to speak. She was placed there to recover through speech and physical therapy. It is a very slow process, but Betty Ann is determined to regain her abilities. For now, though, she is stuck in a wheel chair. Her sagging face muscles and weakened limbs made her dependent on others for care. Gazing out the window, Betty Ann recalls a time when her life held many adventures and she was a beauty. That was so very long ago.

******

"Betty Ann!" The voice bellowed from the garden outside the small house and carried throughout the neighborhood. "Betty Ann! How many times do I have to warn you about climbing on the rose trellis! You are going to break it to pieces and then the roses will have no where to climb. You don't want the roses to lose their way, do you?" A large but gentle man plucked the youngster from the trellis, tossed her into the air, and caught her with his big calloused hands.

"Do it again, Daddy! Do it again!" Betty Ann squealed with excitement, catching her breath. She was the youngest of three daughters born to John and Mary

Christiansen in Briarwood, Nebraska and was always looking for a new feat to try.

"Your Momma would tan your hide if she caught you climbing on her rose trellis, you know that! I'm going to have to build something better for you to do your climbing on," John Christiansen said, lowering the little girl to the ground.

"Daddy", Betty Ann asked innocently, "where would the roses go if they lose their way?" Remembering the previous warning from her father, she imagined them wandering aimlessly around the yard.

"Well, don't you know? If they don't have a trellis to climb, they wander the ground and since they have nothing to guide them their thorns grow long and sharp and they turn into icky old weeds!" He wrinkled his nose and tousled the shiny red curls piled on top of Betty Ann's head.

"Ohhhh…we don't need anymore weeds…we have plenty of those. I'll keep off their trellis, Daddy. I promise!" Betty Ann said, looking up at her daddy; her bright blue eyes sparkling.

******

The hot summer sun beat down on the pale pink roses clinging to the broken trellis out side of the nursing home window. "There, there, Betty Ann. What seems to be troubling you? Maybe the sun is too bright here by the window. I'll close the blinds for you," the little nurse aide said, slowly closing the binds. A tear trickled down Betty Ann's cheek landing on the terry cloth bib around her neck; worn to protect her clothing from the uncontrollable drool trickling down her partially numb lips.

✳✳✳✳✳✳

Glenda carefully replaced the yellowed cloth over the brittle rose. "Betty Ann...Her name is Betty Ann...did you hear that Snarly? The scrapbook belongs to someone named Betty Ann and this rose was given to her by her father. Isn't that neat?" But Prince Snarls was unimpressed and jumped from the back of the sofa to the floor where he ventured over to the water dish and pawed at the floating ice cube. Glenda added, "I wonder where she is now...the owner of this scrapbook. I wonder how they were separated from each other...or if she is even still alive. This looks pretty old."

Glenda Ashbury lives in Bakersfield, Colorado, a very small town untouched by the urban sprawl of the city, where she works in a meat packing plant trimming the fat off prime cuts of meat. She's worked there ever since graduating from high school. It was an excellent opportunity back then and one of the best paying jobs around. Just recently she was awarded a gold pin and plaque for her years of dedicated employment. Glenda has more vacation time accumulated than anyone else in the plant because she just never feels she has anywhere she wants to go. Not any more. Not since her fiancé, Donald Martin, died.

"Hey, Sweetie..." Glenda slowly knelt beside the granite marker on the grassy ground warmed by the mid-summer sun. She placed the cane on the ground beside her. A miniature rose bush, planted next to the grave, was finding its way up the tiny trellis propped in the ground. She gently brushed the debris from the engraving on the small stone; allowing her fingers to caress each letter and number presented there:

Donald L. Martin
October 7, 1958 - August 11, 1999
Rider in the Sky

The stone was engraved with a small motorcycle in the lower left corner and a cross in the lower right; symbolic displays of Donald's pleasure and commitment. He had died doing what he loved and Glenda was with him that day.

They wanted to visit Sturgis, South Dakota during Rally Week. A pickup truck crossed the center line on Blue Star Memorial Highway in the Black Hills. Donald chose not to wear his helmet that day because he loved to feel the wind in his long, partially graying hair. Glenda chose to keep hers on. They were both thrown from the bike. Donald was crushed between the truck and his bike and hit his head after being thrown to the pavement. Glenda saw his body lying motionless on the hot pavement from the grassy bank where she landed. Crawling to him, she was unaware of the severely injured leg dragging behind her. She held Donnie in her arms as he took his last breath.

The memory haunted her and she had tried to deaden it through overuse of her prescription pain pills. The drugs were an escape and a way to mask the pain from her injured leg and broken heart. Extensive therapy helped her recover from the addiction to her pain pills and function through the mental effects of her emotional trauma. But no one, or nothing, had ever been able to ease the sadness and emptiness Glenda felt since Donald died.

She was alone now except for Prince Snarls. An only child of deceased parents, without any known relatives provided Glenda an excuse to become somewhat of a hermit. Donald's family was angry and falsely believed she was responsible for the reckless behavior of their only son. Glenda convinced herself that she was now damaged goods that no one would want. She believed being single for life was her fate.

Her only pleasure was shopping at the local thrift store and accumulating used bits and pieces from other people's lives. She often referred to it as her new therapy. Somehow, it helped her feel like she was part of someone or something. Glenda's life seemed void of any purpose or meaning…until now.

"I found something unique at the thrift store, Donnie," Glenda spoke to the air surrounding her loved one's grave. It just made her feel better to do so. Not that she expected him to respond, but she wanted to believe he could hear her. "It's an old scrapbook and it's full of stuff from this girl's life. Her name is Betty Ann and she traveled to California with her mother and sisters. But I haven't gone any farther in the book to know much else. I've decided to just savor one or two pages a day. I wonder if she is still alive. This may sound crazy, but if she is alive, I'd love to reunite her with her scrapbook…what do you think?" Glenda smiled at the thought of even asking that question; as if Donnie would really answer her. She placed a kiss from her hand to Donald's marker and said, "I'll be back soon." Getting up and brushing the dirt from her knees, she added, "I'll always love you, Donnie." Slowly she turned, leaned on the diamond willow cane, and walked away.

2.

The Colorado evening was cooling down nicely as Glenda and Prince Snarls sat together in the old wooden swing on the large porch. Glenda rubbed the big cat's neck while he purred affectionately. The sun was setting when Glenda lifted the scrapbook from the rattan table and turned the page.

An old black and white photo slipped off the page and onto the cushion. The adhesive, which had held it in place, was yellow with age. The spot where the photo was positioned revealed the original dark gray color surrounded by the exposed faded space. There was a message written on the page in blue crayon that read:

This is how it all began!

Glenda carefully lifted the photo from the cushion and laughed, "Look Snarly, it's a picture of a little circus...and...are those mice on the miniature equipment?" Glenda brought the picture closer for a better look. "I'll be darned. They are mice! And look - there's a Ferris wheel...and a tight rope...how funny!"

Standing in the photo, behind the performing rodents, was a little light haired girl; smiling from ear to ear and leaning her face on one hand, while her elbow rested on the table. Glenda turned the picture over and written on the back was the message, *Betty Ann and her performing mice.* Attached to the same page was a hand written flier on thin yellowed paper:

Come one! Come all!
See the performing circus mice!
Saturday 2:00 pm

At the corner park
ONLY Five cents admission!
FREE POPCORN!

There were hand drawn illustrations of little mice on trapezes and tight ropes. Balloons and flowers were strategically placed around the edges.

"Wow, Snarly, I bet you would have enjoyed this performance!" The big cat glanced sleepily at Glenda, disturbed that she had stopped rubbing his neck. "This Betty Ann was quite the little entertainer. I wonder who made the set for her acrobatic mice."

******

"EEEEEEK!" The shrill cry echoed from the utility room and carried through the halls of the Briarwood Hills Nursing Home. "A mouse! Did you see it! That little rascal just scooted right by me! Where did you go, you nasty little thing!" The night cleaning lady was determined to catch the little varmint which eluded her every move. A nursing home was no place for a mouse, but being surrounded by corn fields, one was bound to find its way into the place.

Betty Ann sat quietly in the hallway, positioned in her chair, observing the whimsical scene. Unable to move freely or express herself, she simply sat there watching, remembering and smiling on the inside. Her outside posture remained slumped and non-responsive. There was a twinkle in her eyes though as she reflected on a past memory.

******

"Oh Daddy! It's wonderful!" Betty Ann shrieked, opening the plain brown box revealing the miniature circus menagerie.

"Happy Birthday, Honey," John Christiansen said to his little girl, "I wanted to get you something special...and well, I hope you like it."

Times were hard for John and Mary Christiansen and their family; as they were for many during the 1930's. They didn't have much money left after the stock market crash. And being a shoemaker wasn't supporting the family adequately.

John was a good man, but a stubborn one and would not leave his life's work for other jobs. So Mary decided to teach her daughters how to perform in an attempt to bring in additional income. Two of her girls were gifted in acrobatic moves and Betty Ann, especially, enjoyed entertaining the crowds. No matter how bad things were, people continued to pay money to be entertained. They still sought pleasure through the depression. Mary knew this, so she started the process of training her daughters. She designed and sewed costumes from fabric which was given to her in trade for mending work. The girls practiced their routines under the strict guidance of their mother. The third daughter, Ida Mae, earned extra money waiting tables at a local restaurant. Once Betty Ann and her older sister Stella perfected their routines and antics, they took their show on the road - performing at local county fairs and festivals across Nebraska and Iowa.

But it all started with the mice. John had acquired some white mice. (A trade for some shoe repair work). Betty Ann loved the little mice and started teaching them how to do tricks by rewarding them with bits of cheese or bread. John, noticing his daughter's natural ability to train

15

the mice and her willingness to perform, built the circus for her as a gift. Betty Ann had those mice doing amazing things and people would pay to see them perform. In those days a nickel went a long way and Betty Ann was contributing to the support of her family.

The funny thing was, when they decided to go on the road to perform, John (being the soft hearted man he was) could not destroy the mice. So, he turned them loose in the basement. The next spring they had the only black and white mice in the neighborhood! Those silly mice remained tame and would swim out across the concrete fish pond after tossed crumbs.

✶✶✶✶✶✶

"Hey, Betty Ann...did you see that little mouse run by here? They ain't no good for nothin'!" The cleaning lady exclaimed, gently brushing her palm across Betty Ann's arm. Betty Ann attempted to smile for she knew better. God had a plan for every creature, big or small. But she often wondered what His plan was for her; especially now, in the shape she was in. Sometimes she wished He would just come and take her home and away from this place.

"Hi Mom...I'm so sorry I am later than usual. We had a crisis at work and I had to stay a little longer." Betty Ann slowly lifted her head so her eyes could meet the eyes of her son and only child, Mark, as he kissed her forehead saying, "Did you have a good day today?" Betty Ann tried hard to make a smile for Mark forcing the one side of her lip to move upward very slightly. "That's my girl!" Mark said as he patted her hand, "Shall we get some supper? I am really hungry...how about you?" Mark stepped behind her chair and whisked her toward the kitchen dining area.

"Hey, Mark, how's it going?" A young table assistant asked as Mark positioned his mother at their table. Mark just smiled back politely as the assistant filled their glasses with water and then retreated to the kitchen. "I can not believe he is here every night to eat supper with her! Doesn't he have a life of his own?" The young assistant spoke softly to one of the aides.

This *was* Mark's life. He took care of and watched out for his mother. Oh sure, she was in the nursing home, but he still felt he had to be there for her everyday. He didn't mind though because he loved his mother and always believed she was an amazing woman. She took care of him all the years he was growing up and now it was his turn to care for her. It was that simple.

"Did you have therapy today, Mom?" Mark asked, taking a sip from his coffee. Betty Ann nodded her head in a positive response. "That's good. Have they been trying to work with you on your speech?" Again, Betty Ann nodded. Mark reached across the table and took his mother's hand, saying, "Mom, you know they say if you don't talk more you will lose your ability to do so. Can you please try and say something...Anything?" Mark gazed at his mother as she gently lifted her head. Staring straight into his deep blue eyes, she slowly said, "I love you, son." The words were clear and distinct, but that was all. Marks eyes filled with tears as he held his mother's hand, responding, "I love you, too, Mom. It's okay. It'll come with time."

******

Glenda placed the photo back on the page and gently closed the scrapbook. It had been a long day and she was tired. The evening air was cool with a gentle breeze blowing from the south. The pungent odor of the packing plant hung in the air; a reminder that morning, and work, comes quickly and she should get to bed.

"Come on Snarly, time to go in," she said, rising from the swing. With the scrapbook in one hand and, taking her cane in the other, she gently nudged the big cat. Prince Snarls scooted through the opened door, annoyed by the prodding, and retreated to his favorite position on the back of the sofa. Glenda placed the scrapbook on the old trunk, smiling as she gently brushed her hand across the front cover. "Tomorrow, I will learn more about you Betty Ann," she said softly, retreating to her room.

3.

It was just another day at work, but Glenda felt an eagerness she hadn't known for a very long time. There was something intriguing about Betty Ann and her life and Glenda was looking forward to going home to peruse the scrapbook again. Glenda anticipated turning another page and speculating on the items placed there. She wondered what the full story was behind each significant remembrance and kept imagining what life was like for Betty Ann and her family back then.

"Why don't we ask Glenda to join us tonight?" the new girl on the line stated to the crowd gathered around the picnic table outside the plant. It was lunch break and the same usual crew sat eating their sandwiches and drinking their sodas while Glenda sat at a distance; alone in her car, listening to the CD player.

"Are you kidding?" a loud boisterous voice bellowed from the group. "She is one weird chick! She wouldn't fit in…besides she can't bowl very good with that bum leg of hers," the big blonde reasoned. After observing the questionable looks on the faces of her peers, she added, "It probably would just make her feel worse…I mean…not being able to fit in and all." The others smiled, nodding their heads in agreement while hastily continuing to devour their food.

The lunch breaks were brief at the plant and there wasn't a great deal of time for small talk or any discussions of fairness and compassion. Glenda's isolation wasn't the fault of the other workers because she chose her solitude as part of the protective barrier constructed for her life. If she didn't let herself get involved in other people's lives, she wouldn't get hurt…again. Therefore, she justly earned the title of "weird chick" as she was often called. So, being alone was a normal occurrence for her. But today, sitting in her car listening to The Beatles sing "Hey Jude" on her

19

favorite CD (for the fifth time), she stared at the group gathered at the picnic table and wondered what it would be like to join them.

"What do you suppose they talk about when they gather like that?" Glenda thought as she chewed the slightly soggy tuna sandwich. (Her plastic container of fruit cocktail had leaked again). Most of her conversations took place with herself or with the cat. She didn't even know if she was capable, anymore, of carrying on a functional conversation with another human being because it had been so long since she tried. The last time she had actually conversed with others had been during her intense therapy sessions. When therapy ended, there seemed to be no reason to pursue other opportunities. She had said all she cared to say; talked all she cared to talk. Even occasionally attending Dual Recovery Anonymous groups she rarely spoke and usually opted to pass when the opportunity presented itself. It seemed easier...safer...less complicated.

"Only four hours left for this work day," Glenda remarked, glancing at the digital clock on the dash of her car. Gathering up the remnants of her lunch and shutting off the ignition, she was suddenly startled by the loud TAP, TAP, TAP on the window next to her head. Turning that direction, she was surprised to see the new girl on the line timidly smiling and motioning for her to open the door. Cautiously Glenda opened the driver's side door.

"Hi! I just thought...maybe I'd come and walk back to the plant with you," the girl said. Glenda could tell by her strong accent that English was not the language she was raised with. She was young, short, dark, and over-weight, but had a contagious smile that she presented to Glenda as she stood there waiting for a response. Glenda had heard that her name was Rose.

Glenda assisted her left leg from the driver's seat and turned, automatically lowering her right leg to the

20

ground. Lifting the diamond willow cane from the passenger side seat, and placing it on the pavement, she used it and the door frame to stand, stating abruptly, "Why didn't you go in with the others?" She turned to close the door of her yellow Volkswagen Beetle; locking it securely.

"I don't know...I guess I just thought maybe you'd like to have some company." Rose said, trying to justify her own need for friendship as the others were constantly pushing her away.

The female workers at the plant could be a cliquey group and it was often difficult for the new-hires to try and fit in. Glenda had observed their coming and going; those who succeeded in becoming one of the group and those who ended up leaving to find work elsewhere. But she never had one approach her this way before.

"Why would you think that...do I look like I need company?" Glenda responded, surprised at the harshness in her voice. It wasn't her nature to be mean, but the verbal response leaped from her lips, automatically, in the same fashion as one would raise their hand to deflect an object thrown at them. It was her defense mechanism; put in place to protect her from intimacy with another human.

"Well, no...I mean...we all need company once in a while. Don't you think?" Rose replied and persisted in walking next to Glenda as she maneuvered the curb of the parking lot to cross the grassy area, which was the shortest way to the plant doors. "I certainly enjoy good company...don't you?" she added.

"I don't have time or need for company in my life right now. You better go ahead or you will be late on your line...no need to wait for me." Glenda responded, coldly attempting to deter this person from her desire for friendship. But Rose was persistent.

"Tell you what...I'll go on ahead, but tomorrow, at lunch, we'll eat together. I'll see you then!" Rose said walking away before Glenda had the opportunity to object. She turned and waved to Glenda; a big smile on her face.

"Little brat! What nerve she has!" Glenda whispered, pulling open the large gray doors to the plant, "What makes her think I'll join her for lunch tomorrow?" Glenda returned to the line to do the job she had always done.

******

"Good afternoon, Betty Ann!" the little nurse aide said, cheerfully entering the room, "We're playing Bingo in the activities room. Wouldn't you like to join us?"

Betty Ann had fallen asleep in her chair with the television channel set on another mindless soap opera. Her eyes opened wide at the cheerful, but annoying, invitation from the intruder into her solitude.

"N-n-noooo!" She managed to moan, shaking her head frantically back and forth in an attempt to be understood. How she hated that game! It seemed so ridiculous for her to sit there pretending to be interested while the nurse aide played the card for her. Actually, she could probably cover the square with the little disk if they would allow her to, and give her a little extra time to do so. But the game was always rushed through; a required entertainment. However, she also despised sitting in her room watching mindless daytime television. How she wished someone would just take the time to read to her. Or maybe she could paint again. She would love to try. She used to love that.

"Oh come on now, Betty Ann. We need to be social. Besides, everybody needs company, don't you think?" the aide said, trying to encourage her patient while straightening her posture and preparing to take her to join the group. "It will do you good to join in with the others. You need a change of scenery."

Experience had proven that it was easier to just go with the flow rather than protest too much. Protesting expended too much energy and Betty Ann was reserving her strength for the visit from her son that evening. Mark always came and had dinner with her. It was the one thing she could rely on and she looked forward to it everyday. As the aide wheeled her briskly to the activities room, Betty Ann thought to herself, "Yes, everyone needs company…even those who reject it."

******

It was five o'clock and Glenda's shift at the plant had ended for the day. As she exited the front door and walked toward her car, a voice called out from the distance, "See you tomorrow, Glenda! Have a good evening!" Glenda paused and turned and there she was; hand in the air and waving. It was the new girl, Rose, smiling cheerfully as Glenda unexpectedly made eye contact with her. Glenda cautiously raised her hand holding the cane in reserved acknowledgement of Rose's kindness. Abruptly she turned away and continued toward the little Volkswagen, thinking, "That kid is way too perky for me."

Prince Snarls was glad to see his mistress as she entered the house and purred at the touch of her hand on his back. He had learned to cautiously circle her legs while staying clear of the diamond willow cane which helped Glenda keep her balance.

"Hi, Snarly. Did you have a rough day?" Glenda spoke to the cat teasingly. She knew Prince Snarls spent most of the day in his favorite spot on the back of the sofa; sprawled out on the old patchwork quilt, and basking in the sun shining in from the bay window. "Oh, to be a cat!" she thought, filling his dish with dry cat food and giving him fresh water. Placing the kettle on the stove, she ignited the burner to heat some water for a cup of tea. She opened the freezer door and stood there pondering which single serving, frozen dinner to prepare that night…chicken, beef or fish. "Thank goodness for Lean Cuisine," she said, lifting the package of chicken with basil and rice from the freezer and preparing it for the microwave. As the kettle whistled, Glenda opened the package of lemon and honey-flavored green tea and placed it in her favorite mug. It was the one Donald had bought for her when they visited Mount Rushmore. It portrayed a cartoon image of the monument from the back side, which revealed four naked butts with legs dangling. There were a couple of tourists staring at the sight and a caption that read:

I think we're somewhere on the back side of Mt. Rushmore!

They both had laughed and laughed at that illustration even though it seemed somewhat of a sacrilege. She smiled down at the cup and breathed in the aroma from the fragrant tea.

After her brief dinner, Glenda retired to the sofa with a second cup of tea and carefully lifted the scrapbook from its place on the old trunk. She turned each page recapturing the joy experienced from the previous revelations…the dried rose and loving note to a daughter from her father...the whimsical photo of the mice circus with the flier announcing the event…and then... turning the next page, she found a chain clinging to it and attached with a piece of yellowed tape. On the end of the chain was a metal charm, revealing just a partial message, as the charm appeared to be broken in two. The letters on the half charm were:

Bes
Frie

As Glenda carefully lifted the necklace from the page, taking care not to disturb the brittle tape holding it in place, she said, "Oh look Snarly. It's a necklace with a charm…well, half of a charm anyway. I'm guessing that the message was 'Best Friends' and that somewhere, someone has the other half of this necklace."

Next to the necklace was an envelope containing a hand made card. Glenda removed the card from the envelope and turned it over, revealing a tender drawing of two girls holding hands. There were brightly colored flowers drawn all around them. The message inside the card read:

Everybody needs somebody, sometime.
I'm glad you are my friend. Good luck on your
adventure to California.
I will miss you. Come home soon!
Best friends forever,
Margie

Carefully sliding the card into the envelope, Glenda noticed something else tucked away inside. It was a lock of light brown hair along with several small black and white photos; like those from an automatic photo booth. There were two girls in the pictures in various poses from serious to silly. The one girl Glenda recognized as the light haired Betty Ann from the picture with the little circus, only she was slightly older. "This must be Betty Ann and her best friend, Margie. Look Snarly, they look so happy…and Margie even put a lock of her own hair in the card." Prince

Snarls was snoozing after his meal and lazily opened one eye as Glenda held up the picture in front of him, attempting to share her moment with someone, saying, "It sounds like Betty Ann was going away…some sort of adventure...to California. This was probably their last fun time together. I wonder how long they were gone."

******

Mark was late again to visit Betty Ann. When he finally arrived at the Briarwood Hills Nursing Home, she was already positioned in her place at their table.

"Mom, I'm so sorry I am late again. Things at work have been so hectic. We have two new clients in today and there is just so much paperwork to process everything." He bent down to give his mother a kiss on the cheek. Betty Ann smiled up at him lovingly and with understanding because she knew very well the struggles and sacrifices one must make to earn a living. Mark tenderly placed the terry cloth bib around her neck and went to check on their meals. As she waited for him to return, Betty Ann's mind drifted to another time in her past.

******

"How long will we need to be gone?" Betty Ann asked, as she watched her mother carefully pack the tapestry bag containing the beautifully handmade costumes she had painstakingly created. They were taking their act on the road.

26

"We will be gone as long as is needed," Mary answered abruptly, "Now, get your things packed." Turning toward the door, she called down the hall, "Stella! Stella Jean! Have you packed your things yet?"

Betty Ann knew the family was having financial problems. The depression had taken its toll on many families. She often heard the muffled tones of her mother and older sister talking together late at night. Sometimes it sounded as if her mother was crying. Her father's business was not currently supporting the family. People weren't ordering new shoes to be made. They could even buy newly created rubber overshoes, which extended the life of the shoe's soles. No one in the Christiansen family was allowed to have a pair of rubber goulashes! The family had also gone to the extreme of renting out their home for additional income and John Christiansen was going to stay in a tent pitched in the yard.

Mary had determined it was time for her to take action. She knew her girls were ready to perform professionally as they had been performing for local dignitaries and at the various county fairs. Even though times were tough, people still paid good money to be entertained. Since John wouldn't budge on his way of making a living, she would have to do something, other than her occasional mending, if their family was going to survive.

"Ida Mae, did you put the screened tent I made in the car?" Mary asked her oldest daughter as she loaded the tapestry bag and her sewing basket into the trunk, which was filling up quickly with all they may need for traveling across country.

"Yes, mother. I think we have everything, except I haven't seen Betty Ann. She was supposed to finish packing her suitcase, but it is still lying open on her bed." Ida Mae stuffed another bag into the trunk.

"Darn that child!" Mary was frustrated with Betty Ann's resistance to the family's survival plan. "Go see if you can find her! We have got to get on the road. The girls are scheduled to perform tonight at the Hall County Fair and you are set up to work the dinner tent. We need to get a move on if we are going to make it in time!" Ida Mae obediently went to search for her little sister.

"I'll miss you, Betty Ann. I made this for you and there is something inside to remember me by. Will you write to me?" Margie hugged her friend closely and handed her the envelope. "Don't open it until you're on the road. Hopefully it will make you laugh!"

Margie Bryant and Betty Ann had grown up next door to each other. They were the best of friends; pledging allegiance to their friendship for life through their very own blood sister's ceremony. Betty Ann poked her finger and Margie poked hers then they rubbed the fingers together promising to be forever friends...blending their blood.

"I have something for you, too. It isn't much, but I won it at one of the county fairs we worked and I thought it was kinda' neat," Betty Ann said, reaching in her shirt pocket and pulling out the chain with the half charm attached. "See, my charm matches up with yours and together it reads, "Best Friends"...we will always be that, Margie...even if I am a zillion miles away!" As the two girls hugged, they heard a voice calling in the distance.

"Betty Ann! Betty Ann! You need to get home...it's time to leave and Momma is about to tan your hide! You still need to finish getting your bag packed...NOW!" Ida Mae was approaching rapidly.

"I guess it's time to hit the road! You take care, Margie! And keep tabs on that good looking brother of yours! Maybe by the time I come back he'll finally notice me! I'll write when I can!" Betty Ann said, running toward her sister and waving good-bye to her best friend, Margie, who was left standing alone.

As Betty Ann entered her room and saw her mother sitting on the side of the bed. "Betty Ann, I know our having to leave is difficult for you to understand, but maybe, if we can think of it as an adventure, it will make it easier. I have something for you," Mary said, handing Betty Ann a package wrapped in brown paper and tied with string, "Open it up, honey."

Betty Ann quickly released the string bow and tore open the paper. Inside was a beautiful scrapbook. Looking at her mother, she said, "Momma, it is soooo beautiful! Thank you!" Mary took her daughter's hand, saying, "Your father made the covers for it and I have included some tape and the corner holders for pictures, which I hope we'll be able to afford to take as we go. There is also some extra paper, pens, and a small paint kit; as well as your mice circus pictures. It will be our record of your performances and this difficult, but adventurous, time. You can put anything you want in it, okay?"

Since Betty Ann was the youngest, Mary knew she was having the hardest time understanding the reason they had to leave. She thought the scrapbook would ease the heartache for her...for all of them. It would be a good record of all they experience the next few months and a good way to keep her daughter content.

Betty Ann brushed her hand across the smooth, tan, leather cover of the scrapbook. She looked into the tear-filled eyes of her mother and said, "It will be okay, Momma. You're right...it's an adventure...and we'll be back soon. I will do everything I can to make sure of that...even if I have to dance and perform 'til I drop!" She hugged her mother and finished her packing, carefully placing the scrapbook and accessories inside her suitcase. Mary stood at the doorway, observing her youngest daughter with love and pride.

As the Pontiac coup pulled out from the driveway, John stood on the sidewalk, outside the little tan house on

Maple Street; waving good-bye to his wife and daughters. A tear rolled down Mary's cheek but she wiped it away briskly. Betty Ann gazed out the rear window at the lonely image of her father. She held two envelopes in her hands; one from her father, the other from her best friend and stared silently at both; debating which to open first. Opening the one from her father, she discovered inside a freshly pressed pink rose from the trellis which was placed alongside the house. There was a note from her father that read:

**Don't lose your way. Find your trellis, Betty Ann.
Love, Dad**

Tears filled her eyes as she recalled the memory of her father's large hands safely removing her from the trellis she loved to climb when she was small, and the story he told her of the wandering roses. Now she was that wandering rose.

She opened the second envelope from Margie. As she pulled out the card, a lock of Margie's hair and some small photos scattered across her lap. When she picked up the photos she laughed. What fun they had that day in the photo booth at the fair! Caressing the soft brown lock of hair, she gently placed it back in the envelope. After reading the message inside from her forever friend, Betty Ann grasped the chain and charm around her neck and stared out the window as the familiar scenery became less familiar. Her adventure had begun.

******

"Mother? Are you all right? You seemed so far away." Mark said, returning to their table with two cups of coffee; one cooled and specially thickened to prevent uncontrolled choking. Betty Ann looked across the table at her handsome son who strongly resembled his father. "I'm f-f-fine, s-s-son," she managed to say...then added, "Th-th-thank you f-f-for the c-company t-t-tonight."

Mark reached across the table, surprised by the clarity in his mother's voice, and taking her hand in his, replied, "Everyone needs someone, sometime...I'm glad I have you. Thank you for the company, Mom." Betty Ann squeezed his hand affectionately.

******

Glenda carefully replaced the note, pictures, and lock of hair in the envelope and tenderly closed the scrapbook. As she brushed her hand across the smooth, tan, leather cover, she wondered what it would be like to have such a friend. Then she remembered Rose and smiled recalling her bold invitation to join her for lunch tomorrow. "Maybe she isn't such a little brat...I mean...after all...everybody needs somebody...sometime," she remarked, sipping her tea and smiling. For the first time in a long time Glenda was actually looking forward to going to work. Tomorrow she would try to be nicer to the new kid on the line.

4.

"Hey, Glenda, where would you like to sit and eat our lunches?" Rose said, approaching Glenda and the doors to the outside. The other women glared suspiciously but Rose ignored them; focusing on catching up with Glenda. She overheard the loud mouthed blonde say, "Who does she think she is… our new little social director?" While the others laughed. But it didn't matter to Rose. She had been laughed at before.

"I usually just sit in my car, listening to music…but I guess it doesn't really matter." Glenda responded. Glenda still wasn't sure about making this connection, but somehow the note on the page in the scrapbook last night inspired a confidence in her she had forgotten she had.

"Why don't we just sit over there on that bench?" Rose said, pointing to a park bench in the landscaped area of the grounds away from the others, "Unless you want to listen to your music…I guess we could just sit outside of your car, but the pavement could be a little uncomfortable to sit on." She was trying to be considerate of Glenda's difficulty with her leg.

"The bench is fine. I really don't need to listen to my music, anyway. It was just something to do." Glenda turned and walked the pathway to the bench. "At least it isn't windy today," she said, attempting small talk.

As they positioned themselves and their lunch bags on the bench, Rose turned to Glenda and asked, "So what kind of music do you listen to?" She took a bite of her sandwich.

"Oldies mostly. You'll probably think this is strange…but I like to listen to "Hey Jude", by The Beatles…over and over…I don't know why. I just really like it. It triggers a good memory of when I was young." Glenda smiled, remembering how her mother and father

32

would sing that song together. Glenda thought it was really a song about St. Jude, the Patron Saint of Hopeless Cases.

"Hey, that's cool…I do the same thing with certain songs and I really enjoy all the oldies. I agree that certain songs can really inspire a memory…some good…some bad." Rose was suddenly silent as she thoughtfully chewed her sandwich.

Glenda could tell there were painful memories lurking behind those thoughts and dark brown eyes. Reaching into her lunch sack, Glenda said, "I try to listen to the music that makes me feel good. It helps me get through the bad times. You want a cookie? I brought some extra." This conversation thing wasn't as difficult as she thought it would be. In fact she was really enjoying the company.

"Yum…thanks…they look good. Did you bake these?" Rose helped herself to the chocolate chip cookies in the plastic baggie.

"Nah…I'm not very domesticated…but I do like fresh cookies so I buy them at the bakery. That way I get just a few at a time," Glenda responded, taking a cookie for herself.

"Do you live alone?" Rose asked, sipping from her can of Coke.

Glenda was surprised by Rose's nonchalant way of asking about her life, but she determined it was innocent enough. "Yep, just me and…well…my cat…Prince Snarls," Glenda said, smiling.

"Prince Snarls! That's a hoot! What a cute name for a cat. How long have you had him?" Rose asked, laughing.

"Gosh, I got him when he was just a kitten. He was a gift from…well, from my fiancé." And Glenda looked away as she took a drink from her bottled water. "It was a long time ago…I guess he'd be almost seven years old now."

"A fiancé, huh? Lucky you…I haven't found anyone I am that interested in…or rather they haven't found me. When did you getting married?" Rose seemed genuinely happy for Glenda.

"I didn't…well, we couldn't. He was killed…a long time ago…"

Glenda didn't get a chance to finish before Rose interrupted, "Oh my gosh! I am so sorry! I didn't mean to make you feel bad…I mean…I hope you know that…me and my big mouth!" Rose slapped her hand upside her head.

"It's okay…really…I've worked through it…for the most part. It was hard though. He was really a great guy. We had so much fun together," Glenda said, smiling at Rose to try to assure her. "He died in a motorcycle accident about six years ago," Glenda answered, anticipating the next question, "What about you? Do you have family around?" Glenda redirected the questioning.

"Me? Oh, yeah, bunches… aunts, uncles, cousins…we all hang out together. My parents work as custodians and I have five little brothers…can you imagine? They can be a real pain in the butt, but I love them. How about you? Do you have family around?" Rose was good at redirecting also.

"Nope. My parents died a few years back. They had me late in life. I was an only child and there are no other relatives around, that I know of," Glenda stated, finishing her bottled water.

"Wow! That has to be strange…being the only one. I have no idea what that would be like. The Martinez's are everywhere…that's my last name…in case you didn't know. You want some apple slices?" Rose handed the container of green apple slices to Glenda.

"Thanks…yeah, sometimes it is a little strange…and lonely." Glenda helped herself to the slices. "This has been nice though…I mean just talking with you.

I'm not real good at socializing. I appreciate you being such a persistent little brat!" Glenda said, smiling and bumping Rose's shoulder with hers.

"Hey, no problem! I just figured you could use a friend as much as me. The others aren't very nice, you know...especially to someone who is...well...different...like me." Rose smiled back.

"Like me too," Glenda said, holding out her bum left leg, then adding, "But that's another story. You know...sometimes...I feel like someone from a carnival freak show!" She glanced at her watch then added, "Hey, we'd better get back inside and on the line. This was fun. Maybe we can sit together again tomorrow?"

"Sure...that would be great...you bring the cookies and I'll bring the fruit! Rose said smiling, "I look forward to talking with you again. Us *freaks* need to stick together!" The two women walked back to the plant together, laughing, as friends.

That evening Glenda opened the scrapbook to the next page which had some torn carnival tickets, an old, stiff deflated balloon, and a flier which read:

CHRISTIANSEN SISTERS
CONTORTIONISTS
AND
ACROBATS
These young sisters, Stella Jean and Betty Ann, present an interesting performance of a difficult act, combined with
SINGING AND DANCING
Appearance Rates at Request

STELLA JEAN WILL SIT ON HER HEAD WHILE STANDING ON HER HANDS
As reported in Robert Ripley's "Believe It or Not"
August 1, 1939

On the opposite page was a hand written note which read:

These are some things and pictures from our jobs with the carnivals. I really liked running the Balloon Dart Game. Stella likes all the attention she gets from performing on stage…especially from the boys…but I think they are yucky…my heart belongs to T.B.!

Betty Ann had drawn hearts around the initials T.B. There were small, slightly yellowed, black and white photos attached to the page with the little black corner holders. Each photo had a hand written caption underneath it describing who was in the picture and where it was taken. The images were quite astonishing.

"Oh my!" Glenda looked at the photos in amazement. Prince Snarls jumped from the back of the sofa alarmed. "I can't believe this! She is literally sitting on her head while standing on her hands!" Glenda was looking at a picture of Stella Jean. "And look at this one! Here they are together…Betty Ann and Stella Jean…look Snarly…they are lying on their stomachs with their legs over their backs and their feet around their chins! Holy Cow!" Glenda had never seen anything like that before. "And I thought I was a freak in a carnival show!" (Remembering the comment she made to Rose earlier that day) and continued, "I can't believe the human body can be put in those positions! This is too much!" The pictures were astonishing and Glenda was amazed at the abilities Betty Ann and Stella had.

It was still early in the evening, so Glenda put the scrapbook away and headed to the bakery department at the local grocery store to get her fresh cookies to share with her friend. Driving back toward her home she thought, "That Betty Ann was amazing! I wonder where she is today. She needs to get her scrapbook back."

******

It was County Fair time and since Briarwood was the county seat, the town was bustling with activities. There were booths and tents with crafts and various vendors anxiously displaying their wares to those strolling by. The carnival was in town with the colorful midway of brightly colored stuffed animals, posters, and various other prizes to tempt the crowd into spending their money and trying their luck. The children were lining up to purchase tickets for the fantastic rides.

"Here, Betty Ann, we'll park you here, in the shade, by this game so you can watch all the people. Do you like the carnival?" The little nurse aide had no idea, and Betty Ann just smiled as she watched the Ferris wheel turn; listening to the shrieks of the children fade in and out with each rotation. The little aide assisted other residents to shady spots to watch the crowds. Occasionally, over her shoulder, she would hear the loud, "Pop!" from someone fortunate enough to hit the evasive balloon with their dart as the Carney coaxed them to try, "just one more time". She breathed in the aroma of funnel cakes, cotton candy, hot dogs, fried onion blossoms, and potato ribbons, and recalled a similar time long ago.

******

"Okay, girls, now this is how it's done. You blow the balloons up just barely full of air, so that they are still soft…like this…" Mary exhaled into the small red balloon filling it and tying the end in a knot. Then she handed it to Betty Ann and Stella so they could feel how she wanted the others to be inflated, saying, "The reason we don't fill them up tight with air is because that would make them too easy to pop. This way the dart just might bounce right off and not break the balloon…it only counts if the balloon is broken." Mary had observed the other Carneys and learned their tricks for the dart balloon game. She continued, "Also, when you demonstrate how to throw the dart, be sure to throw it hard and straight at the balloon…like this…then as the dart approaches the board, the air from the speed of the dart will make the balloon move out of the way…and they will be less likely to pop the balloon. Most people don't realize that if you just lob the dart easily…like this…at the board, it will come down directly on the balloon and is much more likely to pop it," Mary explained while demonstrating each type of throw to the girls, "That is the trick to the game. As long as no one figures this out we will make money. Remember…for every prize you have to give away, it's money out of our profits to replace it…and we want to make money…not lose it!"

Stella and Betty Ann were performing their contortionist and acrobatic act often, but sometimes there was a lull in shows so Mary decided that they could make additional money with a dart balloon game in between acts. The girls really didn't mind though, because it was an opportunity to rest from the constant rehearsals and perfecting of new ways to pose their bodies in bizarre positions.

Betty Ann preferred clowning around with the crowds, singing and dancing over the contortion act, but Stella was a natural at bending her body and limbs in any direction. Stella actually gained some fame and was featured in " Ripley's Believe It or Not" and Robert Ripley himself stated she was the only person in the world who could sit on her head while standing on her hands.

Mary paid to have some fliers printed up to post all over the towns they traveled to and people often came from all around to see the girls perform. Sometimes they would throw money up on the stage after the performance and Betty Ann would dance around collecting it. Ida Mae would help her mother create and repair the costumes for Betty Ann and Stella Jean. She spent her days working in the food tents and serving meals for the crowds. The women would pool their money together at the end of the day and, although money was still tight, Mary was able to save a little, after expenses, and after sending some home to John. She kept the savings in an old sock inside her sewing kit.

******

"Well, Betty Ann, we should get you back to Briarwood Hills, now before the Carneys decide to put you to work for them," the little aide teased, releasing the brake from the wheel chair and pushing Betty Ann toward the van. "I hope you enjoyed your time at the carnival." Betty Ann just smiled, knowingly; her eyes sparkling.

5.

"Are you two *girlfriends* rendezvousing for lunch again today?" The big mouthed blonde announced as she waltzed through the doors. She had an entourage of female workers following closely at her side, laughing at Glenda and Rose as they passed; headed toward their perspective places on the meat line. "I think you are meant for each other!" she added, tossing her head and laughing.

"Stupid witch!" Glenda whispered under her breath as the tall blonde and her cronies strolled past. Glenda wasn't prone to that sort of name calling but she couldn't think of any other word that fit. "She sure thinks her crap don't stink, doesn't she?"

Rose just laughed, "Ah, don't let her bug ya. She is just a big loud blonde with oodles of insecurities…but she's harmless." Rose didn't like the way the others had talked about Glenda when she sat with them around the picnic table. She didn't like being associated with them and was glad that Glenda and she had become friends. Taking Glenda's arm in hers she laughed and spoke loudly so the others could hear her, "C'mon Sweetie. The meat awaits!"

Laughing, Glenda leaned against her cane to recover her balance, "You crack me up!" She said as they walked toward their places on the production line, "See you at lunch break, Squirt!" Rose went one direction as Glenda went another; to the places where they would start their day's work.

At lunch break, Rose asked, "You ever get scared, Glenda?" As she stared off toward the plant. Something was obviously bothering her.

Glenda had noticed, during morning break, that Rose had taken a phone call and seemed very upset while she talked to whoever it was on the other end of the line. "Yeah, I've been scared before…I still get scared

40

sometimes. I think we're kidding ourselves if we say we don't," Glenda replied, trying not to pry into Rose's life. She figured if there was something Rose wanted to share, she would. Her main focus was to just be her friend. "You want a cookie? I made a special trip to the market last night just to make sure I brought them," Glenda said, handing the bag of cookies to Rose.

"Thanks…they look good. I don't know…I'm probably worried about nothing," Rose replied, shaking her dark hair and taking a deep breath, "It is such a beautiful day today! I really like it here. It is the best place I've lived so far."

Glenda looked around at the grounds of the plant surrounding them and the houses in the distance, saying, "I wouldn't know what to compare it to. I've only lived here…all my life. I've only been away once when…well, let's just say six years ago." Glenda was wondering how many places Rose had lived and why. But she wasn't going to ask. Rose had a secret and Glenda wasn't sure she wanted to know anything about it. Knowing would mean getting involved and getting involved meant risking pain. She didn't want any more pain in her life.

The rest of the lunch break was quiet except for the occasional interruption of small talk. Before they got up to go back inside, Rose turned to Glenda and said, "You know…I'm really glad I met you. You are a very special person Glenda Ashbury. God has a plan for you…you'll see. Someday you are going to be so happy."

Glenda wasn't quite sure what to say and could only manage, "If you say so…I'm glad I got to know you, too. You've helped me realize that everybody needs somebody, sometime. You are a good person, too, Rose…always remember that."

When they went back into the plant, there were some men in dark suits waiting to speak to Rose. The plant shift supervisor was with them along with the management team. When Rose came into the building they approached her and escorted her into the office. Before she went through the doors Rose looked back at Glenda and smiled. It was that same smile Glenda remembered from the first time they met, when she tapped on the driver's side window of the Volkswagen Beetle. Glenda raised her left hand and cane in a waving gesture and returned the smile, but inside she was concerned. Rose didn't come back to the line that day.

After work, Glenda overheard the other women saying that Rose and her family were in trouble for working without green cards. It was all Glenda cared to hear. She didn't participate in gossip. Walking to her car, Glenda remembered what Rose said about God having a plan for her and she wondered what his plan was for Rose. She hadn't prayed in a long time, but she took a minute to ask God to please watch over that little Spanish Rose. Then, it started to rain.

"Hi, again, Donnie," Glenda said, standing in the rain staring at the stone on the ground in front of her; the rain dripping off her nose and cheeks, mingling with her tears. She needed to come to this familiar site. There was this emptiness inside her as she spoke to the air, "She's gone Donnie…my friend, Rose. I had forgotten how good it feels have another human being around to talk to and laugh with. I will miss her. I miss you. I just never realized how much I want companionship again…I guess everybody needs somebody, sometime. Rose said God has a plan for me. I sure wish I knew what it was…if you know send me some kind of sign, okay?" Then, she laughed, knowing Donnie would be laughing, too.

Prince Snarls tried everything he could to cheer up his mistress when they finished their evening meals. Glenda had left a brown paper sack on the floor and the cat was entertaining himself by darting in and out of it; occasionally peeking up at Glenda to see if she noticed his antics. But Glenda was far away in her thoughts. Grasping her cane, she rose to go to the kitchen. "Maybe a hot cup of tea will perk me up," she said, lighting the burner and putting the old copper tea kettle over the blue flame. Prince Snarls had followed her into the kitchen; purring and gently rubbing across Glenda's legs and around the willow cane. "You want a kitty snack?" Glenda said, opening the end cabinet drawer.

"Meeeeooow!" The cat whined; begging for the treat. Glenda held the nugget below the counter top as Prince Snarls stood on his back legs to retrieve it and retreated to the carpet breaking it into smaller pieces to devour each crumb.

The kettle whistled and Glenda poured a cup of peach flavored green tea. She picked up the scrapbook and tucked it under her arm. "Let's go out on the porch tonight and look at the stars, Snarly." The rain had stopped and the clouds moved on. As Glenda looked toward the heavens, she thought about Rose and Donnie. "Oh, look, Snarly! A falling star! Did you see it?" The cat looked up at his mistress as if to say, "You've got to be kidding!" Glenda just laughed, "Well, I saw it so I get to make a wish. Hmmmm….I wonder what I should wish for? Well, since everybody needs somebody sometime…I wish for somebody, somewhere, someday…somehow." The cat curled up by Glenda's feet and, as she rubbed his back with the foot of her good leg, and lit the candle on the rattan table where the scrapbook lay. Carefully, she turned the pages; past the dried rose, the mouse circus, the necklace and note, the flier and pictures; to the next page in Betty Ann's life.

The background of the page was black and there were small white dots strategically placed across the page. As Glenda studied the design of the dots a realization came to her, "These are constellations…stars, Snarly. Betty Ann has painted star patterns on this page…oh and look…she

43

even included a falling star....see the streak across the sky?" Opposite the page were several photos. One was larger and revealed four figures standing in front of a screened tent of some sort. Under the photo was this message:

The Christiansen Women – Camping

Glenda studied the photos that were carefully placed on the next two pages of the scrapbook.

******

Mary Christiansen had her hands full keeping tabs on three beautiful daughters and the often unscrupulous characters working the carnivals. She was a woman of strong faith and, although some discredited her for leaving her husband and taking to the road, she also held strong moral values. The older girls were constantly testing her tolerance of those values.

"Ida Mae, where is your sister?" Mary said, shaking the shoulder of the sleeping girl, "wake-up, Ida Mae...where is Stella?" Poor Ida Mae had worked a double shift at the food tent that day and was in a deep, sound sleep when her mother came into the tent.

"Mom, is that you?" Ida Mae asked sleepily, "What's wrong?" She reached for the lantern and lit the mantle, releasing a warm glow throughout the small screened tent. Curled up in the corner was Betty Ann, her mouth wide open and breathing deeply; undisturbed by the noises around her. The bedding where Stella usually slept was disheveled and empty.

"That sister of yours is nowhere to be found. Did she say anything to you about where she might have gone off to or who with?" Mary's emotions were torn between anger and fear. She was angry that her daughter defied her rules of staying near the campsite, and fearful that something terrible may have happened to her. "I have searched everywhere for her...no one has seen her...oh, where could she have gone!" Mary was starting to appear panicky.

"Mom, stop! Think...when was she here last?" Ida Mae said, taking hold of her mother's hand, "Stella is a sensible girl. I'm sure there is a simple explanation. Try to calm down." She was doing her best to console her mother, but in the back of her mind she was thinking about the way Stella flirted with the carnival boys...especially Jimmy. He was the boy that ran the Ferris wheel ride. Ida Mae had often seen them talking together alone, in between the game tents. But their mother had warned them about getting involved with the Carney boys, saying they were like the tumbleweeds they had seen on the plains...no roots to keep them in place. They weren't bad people...they just had a different life. Stella knew this...she wouldn't give her heart away to one of them. She was smarter than that.

"Hey, what's going on?" the familiar voice called from just outside the entrance of the tent, "It looks like a party in here!" Stella untied the flap to the doorway of the tent and crawled inside.

"Where have you been young lady?" Mary demanded, turning toward her daughter and taking her arm firmly. The tone of Mary's voice woke Betty Ann from her sound sleep. "Wh--what's happening?" Betty Ann whispered quietly to Ida Mae who was sitting back observing the scene between their mother and Stella. Ida Mae cautiously motioned for her little sister to remain quiet.

"Where have you been?" Mary asked Stella again, squeezing her arm more firmly.
She looked forcefully into Stella's eyes as she waited for an answer.

"Ouch…Mom…that hurts…don't squeeze so hard! My stomach was upset…I had to go to the outhouse! I didn't want to wake you…I thought I could just slip out and no one would notice. I'm sorry, Mom…I'm sorry!" Stella was crying as Mary released the grip from her arm.

"I called for you…I looked everywhere!" Mary was staring hard into Stella's eyes searching for any hint of a lie.

"I was in the outhouse, Mom…on the other side of the camp. I didn't hear you. I'm sorry. Where did you think I would go?" Stella stared back at her mother and then suddenly realized, "Oh, my gosh! You thought I was with one of those Carney boys, didn't you? Mom, how could you even think that? Give me some credit for being your daughter…a Christiansen, for Pete's sake! Sure, some of them are nice and a little cute, but they're not what I want for my life." Then she took her mother's hand and said, "I do listen to you, Mom…and Daddy. I pay attention to your warnings and advice. You do believe me, right?"

Mary's eyes filled with tears as she spoke, "I just couldn't bear having anything happen to one of you girls. You are my life…our life…your father's and mine…I worry about you all constantly. All I want is for us to all be back together again soon. I want us to make your dad proud and help him save our home and business." Then she hung her head and wept, "I am so sorry, Stella…please, forgive me for over-reacting."

Betty Ann watched as her sisters and mother hugged each other. Their light from the lantern cast shadows of their figures in the bushes next to the tent. She had never thought of being afraid until that moment when she heard the fear in her mother's voice. But somehow she knew everything would be okay. There was always that soft voice inside her that assured her of that. Her mother told her once it was her guardian angel watching over her…Betty Ann liked to think it was true. She just knew God had a plan for her…somehow, someway…someday.

"Let's all just pray that we get to California safely and that there will be plenty of work there for us." Mary said, snuggling in between Ida Mae and Stella. As the Christiansen women lay in the screen tent that night, they looked out the side of the tent at the stars in the sky and held on tightly to each other's hands. Mary pointed out the various constellations to her daughters and when they saw a falling star, they all made a wish…probably the same one.

******

Mark arrived at the Briarwood Hills Nursing Home just in time for the evening meal with his mother. As he walked through the parking lot, toward the entrance of the facility, he could hear the sounds of the locust whining in the trees. The sweet aroma of corn growing in the surrounding fields drifted on the damp night air. He was weary from a long day at work; helping others learn how to help themselves and teaching relationship building skills. Many times he wished for someone in his life to practice those skills with; someone other than his mother, although he loved her dearly. Approaching the doors, the glow of a falling star was detected in the peripheral vision of his eye. As he turned to look, he barely saw the final glow of its trail across the sky. Smiling, he said to himself, "I wish…I wish…for someone, sometime, somewhere…she must be out there…if it's meant to be it will happen."

Just then one of the nurse aides nearly collided with Mark as he returned his focus to the door. "Oh, excuse me...I wasn't paying attention," he said as he held the door for the young girl to exit. She smiled politely, nodding as she continued her conversation on her cell phone.

"Sometimes I just feel so invisible...like no one seems to notice me. I wonder why that is..." Mark thought to himself as he approached the dining area and his mother who was patiently waiting there. "Hi, Mom. How was your day today?" Mark bent down to give his mother a gentle kiss on the cheek.

"My day has b-b-been good." Betty Ann said each word slowly and distinctly. Then she looked at her son and smiled. Her muscles were responding to the therapy and she was gradually regaining her communication skills; although her coordination was still not very adept.

"Hey, that's great, Mom. I can tell you have really been working your therapy...and your smile is back...that's great!" Mark squeezed his mother's hand affectionately. "You know what I think we should do tonight after supper? Let's go outside and check out the stars. The sky is so clear tonight. I even saw a falling star on my way in the door."

"D-d-did you make a w-w-wish?" Betty Ann asked her son as she smiled and tried to wink her twinkling blue eye.

Mark smiled at his sweet little mother and replied, "As a matter of fact I did remember to make a wish...but I can't tell you or it won't come true," and he winked back. It was fun teasing with his mother as he used to. He missed that about her these last few months, since her last episode...that's what they referred to it as...an episode. It was just another set-back, according to his mother...another bump in the road.

"I w-w-would l-l-like to s-s-see the st-stars," Betty Ann slowly replied to her son, then added, "after w-w-we eat." Reaching across the table she handed Mark her terry

48

cloth bib so he could assist her with placing it around her neck.

The Nebraska sky was full of stars that evening. Brairwood was a rural community and so the night stars seemed much brighter than they did in the city where Mark worked. Mark wheeled his mother's chair along the path surrounding the grounds of the Briarwood Nursing Home. "Here, Mom, let me adjust the shawl around your shoulders. The night air can get a little damp this time of year," Mark said to his mother as they paused under the great silver maple tree, "Do you remember that time we were sitting out here and that young eagle was up in this tree? All the other little birds were having such a fit until they finally chased it away! That was quite a sight; watching it spread its great wings and fly across the field...remember that, Mom?"

Betty Ann nodded, gazing at the large tree and beyond its branches to the black sky with its sparkling specks of stars. She always loved looking at the stars...ever since the camping adventure in the homemade screened tent that her mother created. "Th-th-there's the B-b-big Dipper," she said to her son as she slowly raised her hand toward the sky, "Thank you, s-s-son for b-b-bringing me out t-t-tonight." Mark gently squeezed his mother's hand and said, "It's my pleasure, Mom."

The stars were slowly disappearing under the heavy cloud cover that was advancing across the Colorado sky. "Time to go to bed, Snarly," Glenda said to the big cat as she opened the screen door to her home, "Tomorrow's another day...another adventure. I'm glad we have more

49

than a screened tent to sleep in; although sleeping under the stars every night might not have been too bad. I wonder what they did when it stormed?" Glenda carefully placed the scrapbook at its place on the old trunk.

6.

"KA-BOOM!" The crash of thunder rattled the pictures on the wall as Glenda woke abruptly from her sleep. "Geez! That was a good one!" she said as Prince Snarles jumped to the bed leaving his place in the living room, "That one was a bit much for you, too, huh?" she rubbed the cat's neck reassuredly. It was Saturday and Glenda didn't have to work, but she decided to get up and make some tea. As she stood at the sink filling the copper kettle, she could see the rain falling heavily on the ground in her small back yard. "This will be good for my flowers and grass," she said, placing the kettle on the flame, "I won't need to water for a while."

Glenda took her tea to the living room and picked up the scrapbook from the trunk. "Let's see what will be next on the pages for Betty Ann and her family," she said as Snarly chose to curl up next to Glenda on the sofa rather than take his usual place in front of the window. The previous lightning and thunder had made the window seat less appealing, for now. Turning past the camping photos and the picture of the Christiansen girls in front of the screen tent, the next page had a faded postcard with "Greetings from the wonderful state of Wyoming" written across the front of it. Betty Ann had crossed out the word "wonderful" and replaced it with "boring" in red ink. There was a note attached to the page and a drawing of a rather rustic looking motel. Glenda carefully opened the note which read:

Well, we are in Wyoming! The weather got really cold and we were in a blizzard! You couldn't see anything but snow for miles and I could tell Mom was scared to death to drive much further in it. We finally saw some light from a motel that was just on the edge of Cheyenne...well, at least it says it is a motel! It certainly

51

isn't like any motels I have seen in the magazines, but it is still a good sight to behold, considering the blizzard and all. Mom says God provided this place for us to give us shelter from the storm. It is all part of His plan for us. The walls inside are unfinished and are covered with messages written by others who have stayed here when they were caught in a storm. We have an old iron bed for all of us to sleep in and there is a wood burning stove for heat. The owner of the motel provided the wood to burn and even though it is rustic, it is warm and dry. I am unable to take a picture of the place because I am out of film for the camera for now, so I decided to try and draw some pictures of what it looks like here and as we head west toward California.

"Wow, that had to be an experience," Glenda said as she folded the note back up to its original form and then studied Betty Ann's drawings. "She is quite the little artist, Snarly. I can't even draw a decent stick man!"

******

"Good morning, Mrs. Bryant. How are you this rainy Saturday?" Betty Ann slowly turned her head to the direction of the door. It was the activities director, Miss Sarah Swanson. On Saturday she visited each resident's room and reviewed her plans for activities for the next week. Betty Ann gave her a lot of credit for at least attempting to make the time at the facility more enjoyable for the people who were now calling it home.

"G-g-good m-m-morning, M-m-miss Swanson," Betty Ann managed to say reaching her hand toward the visitor in her room.

"Why, Mrs. Bryant! I am amazed! You are really progressing in your recovery. It's so good to hear your voice and see you smiling again," she said as she took Betty Ann's outreached hand and gently shook it in a greeting gesture, "As you know, I like to stop by and see if there is anything you would be interested in participating in...as far as activities. I have heard that you are quite an artist. Would you like to be able to do some painting or crafts?" Miss Swanson sat with her pencil in hand, ready to write any suggestions.

"P-p-painting w-w-would be w-w-wonderful!" Betty Ann said smiling, "I used...used to p-p-paint and d-d-draw quite often...w-w-when I was y-y-younger."

"Then painting it is! I will get some canvas, brushes and paints...are acrylics okay? They are easier to use since they mix and clean up with soap and water," she said as she quickly listed the items on her paper pad.

"That w-w-would be f-f-f-fine, th-th-thank you," Betty Ann again reached out her hand toward the hand of Miss Swanson who tenderly squeezed it expressing her concern and understanding. Betty Ann smiled back as tears of joy filled her beautiful blue eyes. Finally, she would be doing something she loved instead of being so bored. She glanced at the rain falling outside her window; remembering a time when she used her artistic talent to record the events in her life.

******

"You have got to be kidding!" Stella said as she entered the small room of the motel. "Mom, look at this place! The walls aren't even finished!" Betty Ann wondered how Stella could possibly complain about the

53

little room. Compared to the screen tent, this would be luxury.

"Well, Stella, I guess we could pitch the tent in the yard for you if you'd rather sleep out there. I mean, it's only thirty-some degrees out and a blizzard. Would that make you more comfortable?" Mary Christiansen had a way of getting a point across to her daughters with just a little sarcasm.

"Okay, okay...I see your point, Mom. I'm just tired, I guess...sorry." Stella walked over to the wall next to the wood stove. "Look here, others have signed their names on the walls and even written messages. I guess we're not the only ones who have been stranded and forced to stay here..."

Mary interrupted her teenage daughter, "Don't you mean found refuge here? A person always has choices, Stella Jean...and you can choose to look at this negatively or positively. I choose the positive. There is enough negative in this world. I feel we were exceptionally lucky to have found this place when we did. God was watching out for us. I don't think I could have driven much further in the blizzard. I am very thankful and you should be too."

Stella didn't comment anymore, knowing her mother was right, as usual. She started reading the interesting comments on the walls and speculating on the reasons why each person who wrote their name ended up at that place. While she was dreaming up her own versions of other's lives, Ida Mae was busy stoking the fire in the stove and trying to prepare a simple meal for them of canned beans, crackers and tea. Betty Ann was busy with her pencils and paints trying to draw the image of the room around her. The camera had run out of film and they wouldn't be able to get some more until they arrived in a city somewhere, so she decided to record their adventure with drawings.

54

"What are you so busy working on?" Stella asked her little sister as she bent over backwards into a perfect back bend. Stella was always working at keeping her body limber for performing. She was far more dedicated at that than Betty Ann was.

"I'm drawing the room here...and the place from the outside. Since we don't have film for the camera, I thought this might be a way to remember it," Betty Ann said as she held the drawing upside down for Stella to see.

"You really want to remember this place?" Stella whispered so her mother couldn't lecture her on being negative again.

"Yeah, yeah, I do...I think it is all part of our great adventure to California. Besides, no one would believe this place if we just told them about it!" she responded, giggling with Stella as she, too, bent over back wards and joined her on the floor, "Maybe I should try and do a drawing of us sometime."

"Nah...we have enough pictures!" Stella Jean answered switching to a handstand and her famous pose of sitting on her head.

"Okay, girls...I know you feel a need to practice, but this room is a bit tight and I wouldn't want one of you to end up against the wood stove. Let's keep it down on the floor and simple stretches for now, okay?" Mary Christiansen warned her daughters as they lowered themselves to the floor.

"Dinner's ready!" Ida Mae called out to the others, "Grab a plate and spoon. I know it isn't much, but it is warm, so eat up." Ida Mae could work wonders in a kitchen...even a make-shift one. She wasn't the stage performer that her sisters were, but she was gifted in her ability to cook and serve others. Together they all made a pretty good team.

"Let's say grace," Mary said to her daughters as they all gathered in front of the wood stove, "Lord, thank you for providing this place of shelter for us. Thank you for giving us each gifts to serve you. Guide us all to do your will and find our purpose in life. Be with those who are not with us, especially our husband and father, John, that he may remain safe and strong. Watch over us during our travel and please help us to earn enough money to return home soon." And they all said, "Amen."

✳✳✳✳✳✳

The thunder storm was ending outside of Glenda's house. As she stepped out on the front porch she could see the clouds breaking in the sky and rays of light were shining down as if the glory of God were coming through and touching the earth below. Glenda stood there admiring the beauty of it all. Looking toward the heavens, she said, "God, what is your plan for my life? Help me to appreciate the shelters in the storms that you have provided for me along the way...Donnie, Rose and even this little scrapbook. I hope if there is anything you want me to do for you that I am able to do it."

Glenda wasn't experienced in spontaneous prayer. She knew the rituals of religious and memorized prayer, but prayer never seemed very personal to her. Sure she had been baptized and confirmed. She even went to mass...not as often as she should...and had occasionally gone to confession. But there was something missing...something personal. Donnie had that. She could see it in his eyes. She watched it leave his eyes as she held him in her arms the day he died. How she wished she had understood what it was before he left her.

"You know what, Snarly? I think I might go to mass tomorrow. It would probably do me good. I need to say a prayer for Rose and her family, anyway. Yep, that is

56

what I'll do." As she turned to go into her house, the sun broke through the clouds revealing a beautiful blue sky.

7.

Glenda carefully maneuvered the steps leading up to the tall wooden doors of St. Francis Church, located on the east side of Bakersfield. Even though it was early morning, the sun was already shining brightly and it was going to be a very hot day. Drops of perspiration accumulated across Glenda's forehead and at the nape of her neck. Her red hair responded to the additional moisture by retreating into gentle curls. As she approached the doorway, memories from her childhood flooded her mind. "It sure seems like these steps were much easier to climb," she thought to herself, remembering how her mother and father would take her to church with them every Sunday. There probably wasn't a Sunday they ever missed...it was a mortal sin to do so.

"Glenda? Glenda Ashbury...is that you?" A voice called from the top of the steps. As Glenda looked up, she could see a smiling woman, dressed in gray and white, coming down the steps toward her. She was small and stooped, but surprisingly agile at descending the wide stairway. There was something familiar about her, but Glenda wasn't sure what it was.

"I bet you don't remember me," the woman continued, "I used to live next door to you on Seventh Street...Oh, it's been years ago." She reached out her hand to greet Glenda.

Glenda looked carefully into the round, pale, blue eyes set into her small, thin face, which was gently framed with wispy snow white curls. "Sister Caroline? Oh, my gosh! Is it really you?" As the two women met on the fourth step from the top, they embraced each other with joy. "What are you doing here?" Glenda asked holding the tiny nun's hand in hers.

"I came back," Sister Caroline said smiling, "I wanted to return to my home parish to retire...so here I am.

Let me help you with the door, Glenda. These blessed things can be so heavy!" Slowly, but steadily she pulled back on the twelve foot wooden door leading to the sanctuary of St. Francis Church, providing a clear and welcoming entrance for Glenda. "Let's visit some more, after mass. I'm so anxious to hear how you have been, Glenda. It's been a very long time, but I've been praying for you."

"Thank you, Sister Caroline...I appreciate that...I need it! I can meet you at the coffee shop on Main if you'd like...I mean after mass of course." Glenda approached the font of Holy Water and dipped her fingers in it, making the sign of the cross from her forehead to her chest and shoulder to shoulder. Sister Caroline, following behind, repeated the spiritual ritual and said, "That would be fine, dear. See you then." She turned to the left, proceeding to the pew at the front of the sanctuary while Glenda retreated to the last pew on the right, carefully genuflecting before entering the row, and slowly kneeling. Her injured leg wouldn't endure extensive kneeling, but she was determined to kneel in prayer before the mass began.

St. Francis was a beautiful Church with its tall arched ceiling and powerful columns supporting the ancient architectural design. The altar was massive and ornate and there were several levels of statues of various saints and angels; each painted in colorful detail and accented in gold leaf. Above the altar and surrounding it were beautiful fresco paintings of more angels and saints in various poses, depicting scenes and stories from the Bible or their personal lives. Along the sides of the sanctuary were three dimensional plaques, each portraying a scene from Christ's life; before, during and after the crucifixion...The Stations of the Cross.

Glenda had forgotten how much she loved her Church. Kneeling and admiring the beauty surrounding her; she felt slightly guilty for being absent from mass for so long. The warmth of God's love and forgiveness and the joy of worship came flowing back into her heart as tears filled her eyes. She was glad she came this Sunday and anticipated her meeting with Sister Caroline following the mass.

The waitress poured the coffee into Sister Caroline's cup while Glenda repeatedly dunked her tea bag into the steaming hot cup of water; gazing down as the clearness gradually turned to a golden brown. Here she was, sitting across from a woman who, next to her mother, had more influence on her life than anyone else...and she didn't know what to say.

"So, Glenda," Sister Caroline stated softly, "tell me about your life." The nun smiled gently at Glenda as she clasped her small aging hands around the warm cup of coffee; her knuckles revealing the bulging signs of arthritis.

Glenda looked up from her cup of tea; not certain where to begin or what she wanted to say. "My life? Uh...well...it's really pretty basic. I go to work and then I go home. That's about it." She continued to nervously dunk the tea bag more rapidly, as if to distract from the conversation.

Sister Caroline placed a warm hand upon Glenda's hand in assurance, saying, "Glenda, I heard about Donald. I am so sorry. I know how much you two loved each other. It must have been a terrible thing to lose him that way, but you know he was a good Christian man...as wild as he was sometimes!" She winked and smiled an understanding smile. Glenda raised her head and smiled back as the tears were pooling in her green eyes. Sister Caroline continued, "Is that how you hurt your leg, dear...in the accident?" Glenda nodded, responding softly, "Yes, it was crushed and hasn't worked right ever since...but, as painful as it is sometimes, it can't compare to the pain in my heart from losing Donnie." A tear gently trickled down her cheek, to her chin and plopped into her cup of tea. Sister Caroline reached up her sleeve presenting a crumpled but clean tissue, handing it to Glenda, causing her to laugh softly and she said, "Sister, you always were prepared for anything!"

"I believe God wants us to be prepared for anything, but to trust him for everything," she responded, smiling tenderly at Glenda sitting across the table. "Are you trusting God, Glenda?" Glenda silently took a sip from her tea as another tear rolled down her cheek. Sister Caroline continued, "You know, dear, it doesn't have to be that complicated. It's really quite simple, actually. Oh, I know the Church likes to put a lot of razzle-dazzle into worship and religion, and those things are good for discipline and unity, but the core of our faith is the hope we have...through the trust we develop...as we allow our personal relationship with God, his Son and the Holy Spirit, to grow and mature within us. It is a very personal thing, Glenda, and one that each person is called to seek. Only then will we truly find our purpose and direction in life. You must try to keep your heart and mind pure and open to receive God's direction. Remember to confess your sins, meditate on his word and pray always...without ceasing."

Sister Caroline could see the hopelessness in Glenda's eyes and she gently assured her, "My dear, Glenda, don't look so despairing. Living a life of preparation doesn't mean you have to become a nun like me! We are called to live in this world, but not to be of this world. Just be yourself, but allow God to fill your heart with his love and your mind with his wisdom and you will do just fine. Don't concern yourself with being perfect...none of us are...God knows I'm not! Trust him...and you will know your purpose and will find your joy."

There was something so soothing in Sister Caroline's aging blue eyes. They twinkled as she spoke and when Glenda looked into them, it was as if she could see the wisdom and gentle spirit God placed there. She remembered that same feeling as she looked into Donnie's eyes; even when he was dying in her arms. "Thank you, Sister." It was all Glenda could manage to say, but it was all that was needed because Sister Caroline could see the acceptance and understanding as she lovingly looked into Glenda's green eyes.

"My goodness, look at the time!" Sister Caroline quickly sipped the last of her coffee. "I am sorry, Glenda, but I really must go. Father has some tasks for me to do yet this morning and I promised to visit another family later today. I'm afraid it is going to be a scorcher today...I can feel it in the air outside...don't you think?" The bright morning sun was shining through the large glass windows of the café, warming the table where they sat. Glenda rose from the table as Sister Caroline scooted across the bench seat of the booth and stood; smoothing out the wrinkles from her gray cotton skirt.

"Thank you for joining me, Sister," Glenda said, retrieving her diamond willow cane from the opposite bench. "I think talking to you was just what I needed today," she continued, smiling and then gently squeezing the nun's hand. "I'm so glad we ran into each other like this."

Sister Caroline squeezed Glenda's hand firmly, saying, "You know, Glenda, there really are no coincidences in life...at least that is what I believe. I feel God puts us just where he wants us for who ever needs us. I'm glad we could be here for each other. You were just what I needed today, too." She handed the young girl at the cash register a five dollar bill, saying, "Keep the change, dear...and God bless."

"Sister, I didn't intend for you to pay..." Glenda spoke up.

"Oh, nonsense!" Sister Caroline said waving her hand, "It's my chance to share a blessing!" And she hugged Glenda as they exited the café. "You take care,

Glenda," she said, turning and waving as she walked briskly down the street, "Remember to stay open to God's direction for your life...and be happy!"

Glenda waved back, watching as Sister Caroline turned the corner and out of sight. "What an amazing little woman," she said. Shading her eyes from the sun, she looked up toward the bright blue sky, "She's right, it's going to be a scorcher today; probably a record high!"

******

Worship services at the Briarwood Hills Nursing Home just weren't the same as attending in an actual church. Occasionally, a local minister would come around and the residents would gather in the commons area to hear a sermon and sing a few songs, but it just wasn't the same. Betty Ann sat anxiously waiting for Mark to arrive and take her to their little church in Briarwood. Gazing out the window, the sun's rays shined warmly upon her. She looked forward to attending an actual church service again and seeing the familiar faces. Reverend Johnson always presented a good message to the congregation and she loved to listen to the choir sing.

"Hey, Betty Ann. How are you?" the little nurse aide asked as she came through the entrance doors, "Are you going out in this heat?"

"Y-y-yes...my s-s-son is t-t-taking me to ch-ch-church today," Betty Ann responded, smiling and smoothing out the cotton skirt that draped over her knees. Her arms were responding much better to the commands of her thoughts and she was able to move them with less shaking.

"He is...well, that's good. I hope it's air conditioned though, because it's hotter than...uh...well...you know what out there!" The nurse aide said, winking and laughing as she walked briskly past Betty Ann and down the main hall.

Looking out the window to the parking lot in front of the nursing home, Betty Ann could see Mark as he parked the blue Malibu. It used to be her car, but was sold to him when she was no longer able to drive. Approaching the home, Mark wiped the perspiration from his brow. "It must be terribly hot today," Betty Ann thought, observing her son, "But I bet it still isn't as hot as it gets in the desert!"

******

Mary Christiansen was concerned as the Pontiac coupe struggled to make its way through the Rocky Mountains. Fortunately, that early snow storm they encountered in Wyoming was all the snow they'd seen so far; except for the occasional white blanket across the highest mountain peaks in the distance. The women continued their drive toward California; stopping only for fuel and the replenishing of supplies for meals. Ida Mae was in charge of preparing the sandwiches that were eaten at the various roadside stops.

Mary had kept a close watch over the money they had earned while traveling with the carnival and from the shows Stella Jean and Betty Ann performed in, as well as the income contributed from Ida Mae's job as a waitress. She carefully calculated the miles yet to travel and the amount of gas the car would need to get to Los Angeles. If they were frugal, they could just make it. At night she would pray for God's protection and that the car would stay mechanically fit. They couldn't afford any additional expenses.

It was dark as they approached Salt Lake City, Utah. Stella was excited and shook Betty Ann's shoulder saying, "Hurry! Look! Oh, golly, it is so beautiful, Betty Ann...wake up and look!"

Betty Ann was sound asleep on the shelf space between the back of the seat and rear window. Since she was so small, it was the perfect area for her to lie down and get some rest. Stella's awakening had startled her and when she attempted to sit up her head was greeted bluntly by the back window, "Ouch!" she said as she rubbed her forehead sleepily, and then she saw what Stella was so excited about. There in front of them were the lights of Salt Lake City, glowing in the distance below as they descended from the mountains. The warm glow was a welcomed sight. "It is so beautiful!" Betty Ann exclaimed and she knew it would be a sight she would never forget.

"We'll sleep here tonight." Mary told her daughters. "Tomorrow we drive toward the desert." The women stayed in a motel, but Stella and Ida Mae hid in the car and sneaked into the room later, when the manager wasn't looking, to avoid having to pay the additional charges for more people; there just wasn't enough money for that. That night Mary asked God to forgive her for deceiving the manager and thanked Him for watching over them on their journey west.

******

Glenda was glad to get home to the air conditioned comfort of her little house. "Hey, Snarly!" she said as she entered the front door. The big cat raised its head, then with his back legs standing, stretched his front legs as far forward as possible; gently clawing the quilt spread across his perch on the back of the sofa. He presented a big, lazy yawn and then jumped down to greet Glenda.

"It's hot out there, Snarly. I think it's the hottest day yet...bet it hits one hundred today!" Glenda gave the cat a gentle rub behind the ear as she sat on the sofa. The scrapbook was on the old trunk in front of her and she picked it up turning to the last page of drawings from the Wyoming motel and snow storm.

Pasted in the center of the opposite page was a post card with a picture of a huge church on the front. Betty Ann wrote a message next to it that read:

This is a picture of the church most of the people in this state belong to. Momma says they are called Mormons. I don't think they believe the same as we do, but most of them have been really nice and friendly. We stayed in Salt Lake City at a motel because it was so late when we arrived and Momma didn't want to have to set up camp. We didn't have enough money to pay for all of us to sleep in the room, so Ida Mae and Stella Jean sneaked in later after the manager wasn't looking and slept on the floor. This post card was free and left in the room as a souvenir. The next day we drove and drove for miles and miles. There were rugged rock formations and then miles and miles of desert. It was so HOT!!!!! Momma was worried about the car overheating. Luckily she brought extra jugs of water when we left Salt Lake City.

As Glenda turned the page, a photo slid from its place and onto the cushion beside her. She picked up the photo and placed it back in the corner holders next to the following message:

**When we got to Boulder City Momma wanted us
to see the famous Boulder Dam. I guess President
Roosevelt was here a while back to dedicate it. So we
drove up the winding road to the dam site. It was so hot
and we took towels and soaked them in water to put on
our heads to cool us off. The water would leave them
before we even got them around our heads because it
was so hot and dry! I didn't care much about seeing the
dam, but I did take this picture. I was just too hot to
care. I just kept thinking about what it must have been
like for the men who built the dam and how hard it
would be to work in this heat. I was glad when we were
back on the road again.**

In the photo were three very weary looking women
standing in front of an old car with a large dam in the
distance. Glenda looked closely at the picture and then
said, "Betty Ann must have taken this. She must have
replenished her film somewhere. Boy, they look hot, don't
they, Snarly?" She raised the photo to the cat sitting behind
her shoulders, adding, "They didn't have air conditioned
cars back then. It must have been terrible driving across
that desert in all that heat. I just can't even imagine! We
are so spoiled these days."

✳✳✳✳✳✳

"Hi, Mom!" Mark said as he entered the doors at
the Briarwood Hills Nursing Home. "Looks like you're
ready to go," and he bent down to give her a kiss on the
cheek. "It's pretty hot out there," he warned her,
maneuvering the wheelchair through the automatic door.
The heat from out side felt like one was entering an oven.
Betty Ann waved her hand and said, "Oh, th-th-that's

67

okay...I-I-I-I've b-been th-th-through worse." Then she smiled, remembering her experience crossing the desert so many years ago.

8.

It was an exceptionally long day at the plant and Glenda was tired and glad to be on her way home. She was tired of cutting meat, tired of the heat, and tired of being alone. "Think I'll stop by the church and see if Sister Caroline is around," she said to herself as she pulled out from the plant's parking lot.

"Well, hello there, Glenda. Didn't I just see you here yesterday?" Father Harris said cheerfully, reaching his right hand forward to take hers.

"Yes, Father...must be some kind of a record for me...I guess." Glenda shook his hand softly, and asked nervously, "Um...I was wondering...is Sister Caroline around?"

Father Harris sat at his desk and was busily thumbing through the day's mail but stopped and slowly looked up at Glenda. "Sister Caroline? No, no she isn't here. Apparently a family member back east became ill and requested her presence. She left early this morning. Is there something I can help you with?" He could see the disappointment on Glenda's face.

"No...not really...I mean...thank you, Father...I just wanted to visit with her. We had such a nice visit after mass yesterday. I just thought...well...never mind. I should quit bothering you on your day off. Do you still try and keep Monday as your personal day?" Glenda remembered that from years before. Often her parents would invite him over for dinner on Mondays.

Father Harris gave a jolly laugh. He always reminded Glenda of Santa with the way he laughed and how his big belly would shake. He smiled up at Glenda saying, "Well, you know how it is. I try to be available when I'm needed. If I get a free day, I consider it a gift. Do you need something, Glenda?"

Glenda was looking down at the floor but raised her head and smiled at the old priest whom she had known for so many years. With a sigh she whispered, "A friend."

The old priest got up from his chair and leaned against the corner of his desk, taking Glenda's hands in his. His gentle eyes gazed into hers and he replied, "Now, that I can be. Tell me what seems to be troubling you, child?"

Glenda squeezed his hands gently then released them saying, "Thank you, Father. I'm fine...really...just lonely...I guess. It's just that...well...lately, I've been wondering just what my purpose is here. I mean, on this Earth...what is it all about? I feel like I am supposed to be doing more...but I don't know what it is. Am I making any sense?"

Father Harris crossed his arms in front of his chest and smiled. Slowing nodding his head, responding, "You are making perfect sense, Glenda. It sounds like God is preparing you for something. It happens that way sometimes. Don't stress over it...just keep your heart open and trust him. You'll know soon. How is work going at the plant?"

Glenda sighed, "Work is fine...the same old thing I've been doing for years. I've been thinking of taking some time off, but I don't know where I would go or what I would do. I certainly have plenty of vacation and personal time stored up...just no clue as to what to do with it."

The old priest laughed again, saying, "Oh, to have such a problem! You should take some time, Glenda. Now would be a good time for you to take some time for yourself...a time to reflect on these thoughts and feelings you are experiencing. Perhaps you would enjoy a retreat. It just so happens that I have received some information about an upcoming retreat to be held at the St. Francis Monastery in Highland. It's here somewhere..." he turned and shuffled through a stack of papers on his desk. "Ah! Here it is...see it says here, 'it is a special retreat for those

70

who are seeking peace and purpose'. Apparently there will be speakers there from other areas of the country. There are even some sessions for those who are recovering from loss or addiction. I have visited that monastery, Glenda. It is a wonderful place to clear one's head." He handed the brochure to Glenda.

"Um...this looks very interesting, Father. I like the idea that it is here in Colorado, also. Gosh, I haven't been to the mountains in ages..."

Glenda slowly turned the pages, scanning the information and highlighting in her mind the topics of interest...*clean rooms...beautiful gardens with reflection pools...prayer and meditation rooms...all meals and snacks provided...optional sessions of instruction in various areas of personal growth or development...opportunity to establish new friendships in Christ.* "Thank you, Father ...It looks amazing...I think this might be just what I need. It certainly is reasonably priced. I'm glad I took the chance and stopped by."

Father Harris smiled knowingly, "You were directed here, Glenda...there are no coincidences in life. Things don't just happen by chance to those who believe...but I'm glad you were willing to stop by, too. You know, feeling the direction is only a part of the process of finding one's purpose. You also have to be willing to do or go as that direction is revealed. But you can't do that without preparation. I think you and God are working to prepare you for something, Glenda. Keep your heart and mind open to the leading and your faith strong." As he walked Glenda to the door he continued, "I'm glad I was here for you, Glenda. I hope this will be just what you need."

"Thank you, Father," Glenda said, giving the old priest a hug. "You were always there...I'm the one who stayed away...but I always knew what I believed in my heart. I am so excited about this. I just know it will be a good thing."

******

At the Briarwood Hills Nursing Home, Miss Swanson the activities director, paused at the doorway to Betty Ann's room, "Oh, Betty Ann! That is such a beautiful painting! Where on earth did you get the image from?" Perched on the easel was a canvas with a beautiful mountain scene. There were the greenest evergreens and wild flowers along the highway winding through the mountain pass and snow capped peaks in the distance. Miss Swanson entered the room, adding, "Is this a place you've been to before?"

Betty Ann was sitting in her wheelchair; palette balancing on her lap and brush in hand. She looked up at Miss Swanson and smiled, "Y-y-yes...many y-y-years ago. I w-w-was j-just a ch-ch-child....b-b-but I remem-m-m-ber it w-w-well."

"I love the mountains...and the wildflowers. Where is it...Colorado?" Miss Swanson asked as she studied the painting closer.

"No-n-n-o...it is actually the m-m-m-mountains of C-C-C-Calif-f-fornia." Betty Ann replied slowly, "One of the m-m-most beautiful p-p-p-laces on this p-p-planet. I l-l-lived near th-th-there once. For a l-l-little wh-wh-while. A l-l-l-ong t-t-time ag-g-go."

"I didn't know you lived in California, Betty Ann. I thought you always lived right here in Briarwood. I hope you can tell us all about someday, but for now, your painting can tell the story...its beautiful!" Miss Swanson patted Betty Ann's arm gently and then left the room.

Betty Ann lifted the brush slowly and filled the tip with the deep green paint from the palette. Carefully she touched the brush to the canvas; filling in the gentle bows of the evergreen tree. The images stored in her memory were taking form on the canvas before her; as her thoughts went back to that special place in time.

******

The Pontiac coup had been so reliable...until now. There was a bang and then steam as the poor car slowly rolled to a stop.

"Oh, Lord! Not now, please, not now!" Mary Christiansen said as she clutched the steering wheel rocking her body forward as if to assist the poor car in its struggle to continue.   The Christiansen women had made it through the desert. They only needed to stop occasionally to add water to the overheated radiator. But now poor Old Blue (as Betty Ann like to call it) just couldn't go on anymore. Something gave way to the heat.

"It's probably the radiator hose." Mary said to her daughters. "Ida Mae, go ahead and get out the sandwiches and water. I'm going to take a look at the map and see how far it is to the next town. Hopefully it won't be too far. At least we are out of the desert now and heading into the mountains. There's a stream, over there, where you girls can cool your feet and freshen up a bit. Just be sure to stay close and keep an eye out for any wild animals.

"Race you to the water!" Stella Jean hollered as she dashed across the road and to the grassy meadow which was dotted with colorful wildflowers.

"No fair! You got a head start!" Betty Ann called back as she chased after her sister.   Once the girls reached the grassy area Stella proceeded to do several cart wheels and stretches. Betty Ann immediately went head over heels and started walking on her hands toward her sister. The cool, soft grass felt good against the palm of her hands. Then they sat on the grassy bank dangling their feet in the cold mountain stream.

"It is so beautiful here, isn't it Stella? It's so good to see the green trees and the flowers and the mountains in the distance. I can't wait to drive farther up in them. Everything is so pretty and the air smells so good...like pine." Betty Ann took a deep breath.

"That's because we're surrounded by pine trees, silly." Stella said as she splashed her sister with the cool stream water.

"Hey, you've had it now!" And Betty Ann jumped into the stream kicking water toward her sister on the bank.

"Okay, Okay...stop! You'd better stop before I get in there and dunk you a good one!" Betty Ann knew her sister would, too, so she stopped.

The girls waded in the water picking up shiny stones, putting the special ones in their pockets, and trying to make the flat rocks skip across the water. They decided to pick a few wild flowers to take back to their mother.

"What does it look like, Momma?" Ida Mae asked as she set the sandwiches on a cloth across the trunk of the car and approached her mother, who was looking under the hood at the steaming engine.

"Well...it looks like a very hot engine!" Mary said laughing. "Didn't we pass a road sign not far back for a service station up ahead?"

"Yeah, I saw that, too. I think it said it was only a couple miles. Are you going to try and walk there, Mom?" Ida Mae was concerned about her making the walk alone.

"Well, let's just sit and think for a minute," Mary continued, "We'll eat our sandwiches and maybe some nice folks will drive by and give us a hand. If not, then I guess

I'll have to do some walking. Why don't you go over and get your sisters, Ida Mae, so we can eat." Mary didn't want her daughters to know the anxiety she was feeling at the moment. She had calculated their money as closely as possible and there was only a few dollars left in the brown sock where she kept it stashed. An expense like this would surely wipe them out. They would also need some money once they reached the city until they found work.

As Ida Mae walked toward the meadow, Mary looked to the sky and prayed, "Lord, please send someone...someone good....to help us. And if it isn't too much to ask, Lord, please have the cost to repair Old Blue not be too great..."

"What you looking at, Momma?" Betty Ann asked, handing her mother the small bouquet of flowers while shading her eyes; looking toward the area of the sky her mom was staring at. "Did you see an eagle or something?"

Mary laughed at her daughter and said, "No...I guess I was just looking for an angel...you didn't see any over there by the creek, did you?" She gave her daughter a hug. "The flowers are beautiful, thanks, honey. Now, let's eat our sandwiches. Everything will be fine."

The women sat and ate their sandwiches on a blanket laid out on the soft grass near the side of the road. Within a few minutes a car slowly pulled up and stopped a few feet away. Mary rose from the ground and instructed her daughters to stay put. She walked toward the car, praying silently. The gentleman stepped out of the car and walked toward her. There was a woman who remained in the front passenger seat.

"You having some trouble?" the man asked as he approached Mary. He was tall and wore a gray suit and hat. "My wife and I saw the moisture on the road back there and I told her it looked like someone might have blown a hose. It happens often when people get through the desert and start up these mountains."

Mary took a deep breath, "Yes, I'm afraid that is what happened to us, too. Do you know how far it is to the nearest station? I thought I saw a sign..."

"Oh, Yeah...that's right...there is a sign now. The station is just up ahead around that curve. Not far at all. Would you like us to give you a lift there? I'm sure they can tow your car and have it fixed in no time. Where are you headed? Oh, by the way...my name is Allen. Allen Johnson and that is my wife Sally." Mary could see the attractive blonde wave to her as she looked toward the Johnson's car.

"It's good to meet you Mr. Johnson. My name is Mrs. Christiansen and these are my daughters...Ida Mae, Stella Jean and Betty Ann. We are headed to Los Angeles but are from Nebraska. I would really appreciate a lift to the station...thank you. Do you think you have room for my daughters, too? I just don't feel comfortable leaving them here by the side of the road." Mary didn't want to impose, but she could see gentleness in Mr. Johnson's eyes and felt it would be okay to ask.

"Of course...yes, we have plenty of room...by all means; we wouldn't want three beautiful young women sitting along side the road. Don't you worry, Mrs. Christiansen, Smitty at the station will have your car up and running again in no time. I'll go tell my wife. You gather your things and we'll get going." He turned and walked back to his car. Mary watched as he leaned into the window, explaining the situation to his wife. She smiled and waved and Mary felt a sense of relief.

"Come on girls," Mary said as she gathered up the blanket from the ground, "Mr. and Mrs. Johnson are going to give us a ride to the station in their car. Help me get the things we need from our car to take with us. Hopefully the station will have a way to tow our car in and repair whatever is wrong with it."

Mrs. Johnson slid over on the front seat next to her husband so Mary could sit in the passenger side. The three girls sat together in the back. Mary turned to the pretty blonde and said, "Thank you so much. I was going to walk, but this is much better...thank you." Mrs. Johnson just smiled and nodded.

The station really was just around the curve, but it still would have been quite a walk. Mary and her daughters exited the Johnson vehicle and they all thanked Mr. and Mrs. Johnson again for their kindness.

Smitty was standing in the doorway wiping grease from his hands on an old rag. "So what can I do for you?" He asked as he spit brown tobacco juice on the ground.

Mary took a deep breath and stepped up to the doorway facing him, "My car broke down just down the road. I believe the radiator hose needs to be replaced. Would you be able to fix it for us?"

"How far down the road is it?" he asked, spitting again and glancing over at the three young women huddled together by the corner of the building. "You girls can sit inside if you like. I got some of them Hollywood magazines in there to look at, if you're interested." He winked at Mary and continued, "They ain't the bad kind...I promise. Just the newsie ones...lots of pictures...help yo'self."

Mary nodded to the girls to let them know it was all right. Betty Ann walked up to her mother and whispered in her ear, "Momma, I need to go to the bathroom."

Mary smiled and whispered back, "Me too." She turned to the mechanic and started to ask, "Mr. Smitty..." but was immediately interrupted.

"The name's Smitty...just Smitty...not Mr. Smitty," the mechanic said with a wink.

Mary cleared her throat and continued, "Well, then...Smitty...do you by any chance have a toilet facility we could use?" She stood with her hands on Betty Ann's shoulders.

"Well, there's an outhouse out back. It ain't much, but I tries to keep it clean. You're welcome to use it...lots of people do." Smitty pointed to the small building behind the garage at the end of a well worn path. There were patches of wood nailed in place to cover large cracks.

Mary could see the look of concern in Betty Ann's eyes and gently squeezed her shoulders. "Thank you, Smitty. We appreciate it." Then she whispered in Betty Ann's ear, "Come along, honey. It can't be as bad as squatting in the woods! I'll go first."

As the women approached the out house Betty Ann looked up at her mother and said, "How much do you think it will cost to get the car working again, Momma? Will we have enough?"

Stopping, Mary turned her daughter toward her saying, "Betty Ann, don't concern yourself over the money. It will be fine. God has watched over us so far. I don't think he's going to leave us now." But deep inside she was wondering the same thing and she whispered a prayer as she opened the outhouse door.

There's just nothing good that can be said about an outhouse. Even though the odor was strong, the small building served a good purpose. And today it served an even greater purpose. There on the floor was a roll of green dollar bills. Mary couldn't believe it. "It must have fallen out of someone's pocket when they used the facility..." she thought to herself, "it could have been anyone...what should I do?"

"Momma, you almost done? I really need to go!" Betty Ann called from outside the door. Mary grasped the money tightly in her fist and replied, "Yes...yes...I'll be right out." She tucked the money into her bra and put her hand to her heart, whispering, "Thank you, Lord."

******

"Hey Snarly!" Glenda greeted her cat companion as she opened the door and placed the brochure for the retreat on the kitchen counter. "How's my fur-ball buddy today!" The big cat purred and rubbed himself against Glenda's legs. "I'm beat, Snarly. I think a need a break from it all."

She picked up the brochure from the counter and took it into the living room; opening it as she sat down on the sofa. Prince Snarls took his place behind her on the patchwork quilt. He looked over her shoulder and gently nudged his face against the side of her head. Glenda reached up to rub his ears and he purred responsively. "Of course if I do decide to do this retreat thing, I'll have to find someone to look after you. I just don't know who that would be." She tossed the brochure on the cushion beside her.

She was tired and her leg was aching, so she propped it up on the old trunk with some pillows. Taking the scrapbook from the trunk, she carefully opened the pages. "I wonder what Betty Ann is up to now," she said as she turned past the page containing the photo of Boulder Dam and the note about the desert heat.

Glued to the next page was a white envelope which was bulging from the objects stored inside of it. Carefully Glenda lifted the flap which was tucked inside to secure the contents. Her fingers reached into the envelope and she felt the cool smooth stones; each one a different shape. They were obviously very special to Betty Ann or she wouldn't have made a special place for them in the scrapbook. There were also several dried flowers taped in place; brown and brittle from age, but Glenda could tell they were probably very beautiful at one time. Betty Ann had also included a sprig of pine, which still contained the faint odor from the sap. On the opposite page Betty Ann wrote:

The California mountains were a sight to behold and it was so good to see things green! Old Blue (the car) broke down and we rode to town with Mr. and Mrs. Johnson. At the service station Momma and I had to use the out house. It smelled terrible! I don't know why, but Momma seemed real happy after she used it. She said it was better than squatting in the woods! The man at the service station had all sorts of Hollywood magazines to look at while we waited for him to fix the car. My favorite Magazine was the one called "PIC". It had a lot of pictures and stories about the movie stars. I wonder if we will see any movie stars when we get to Los Angeles. Momma says we have an uncle that lives there and we might stay with him for a while until we find work and earn some more money. Momma just keeps telling me that God will take care of us. I hope He is taking care of Daddy, too. I miss Daddy. I hope we get somewhere soon so we can start writing to each other. I miss Margie, too. I wonder how her brother, Timmy, is doing and if he even realizes I am gone. I am anxious to see the ocean.

Glenda gently closed the pages of the scrapbook. "Well, Snarly, Betty Ann has had quite an adventure. I can't imagine driving across country like that. They must have had great faith in what they were doing. It was hard back then. People had to go where the work was, but for a woman to go with her children...wow, that took guts." Glenda picked up the brochure from the cushion next to her and then the phone rang. Using the willow cane she got up from the sofa and went into the kitchen where the phone hung on the wall. "Hello?"

"Hello? Glenda? This is Father Harris. Have you thought anymore about the retreat?"

Glenda couldn't believe he was calling her. She replied, "Well, yes, Father. As a matter of fact I was just looking at the brochure when you called. Why do you ask?"

"Oh I don't know. I just felt I needed to call you. Is there any reason why you wouldn't be able to go?" Father Harris didn't know why he was asking; only that it was laid upon his heart to do so.

"Well, the only thing I am concerned about is who I could get to check in on my cat, Prince Snarls. I've never left him before...I guess it's silly, but he is rather special to me. I don't know anyone I could call..." Glenda's voice drifted.

"Well, now you don't need to worry about it anymore. I would be happy to check in on your cat for you while you are gone. I just knew I needed to call you for a reason. You know, everything works out somehow. Shall I register you for the retreat?" Father Harris sounded relieved and happy.

"Thanks Father...yes, I think I should go. I need to step out of this safety zone I've created for myself and learn to trust. I won't ever grow or find my purpose if I don't go for it when I know I should...and I think I should do this," Glenda replied, adding "Are you sure it isn't too late to register? Don't the sessions start this coming weekend?"

"I'll call first thing in the morning. I'm sure it isn't too late, but I'll let you know," Father Harris responded. "You have a good evening, Glenda. Talk to you tomorrow."

"Okay, Father. And thanks again...for everything," Glenda replied.

"My pleasure, Glenda, good-bye," the priest replied.

"Good-bye Father." Glenda placed the receiver back on the base. Turning to the cat sitting on the sofa she said, "Well, Snarly, I'm stepping outside the safety zone. What do you think of that?" The big cat just tilted his head and stared. Glenda looked at the scrapbook and said, "After what I've read about Betty Ann, her mom and sisters and all they have done, I think I can manage getting away for this little retreat!"

9.

The following day, after work, Glenda decided to make a visit to the cemetery to check on the condition of Donald's grave site since the recent thunderstorm. Often the large cottonwood tree, overshadowing the grave, would shed small twigs and limbs after a heavy rain and she wanted to make sure they were cleaned up around his resting place. "Donnie was always such a neat-freak!" she thought to herself as she approached the narrow entrance of the cemetery drive in her yellow Volkswagen Beetle.

It was a beautiful day. The Colorado sky was bight blue above the mountain range, and contained large, fluffy, white clouds that appeared to be absolutely motionless; giving one the impression of looking at a painting. Brightly colored wild flowers dotted the tall green grass surrounding the cemetery lawn, which was normally parched and dry. Glenda parked her car, close to Donnie's grave, and sat for a moment just admiring the beauty presented outside her windshield. Without thinking, she commented, "Wow, the rain has really brought things to life around here!" She laughed at the humor of that statement being made while sitting in the middle of a cemetery, realizing it was just the kind of thing that Donnie would have said.

"Hey, Babe," Glenda said as she carefully bent down to remove a fallen branch from the grave of her sweetheart, "just thought I'd stop by and clean things up around you. We had quite the storm the other day."

One by one she placed the twigs and limbs in a neat pile by the side of the road where the grounds keeper would see them and haul them away. She slowly and carefully lowered herself to the ground and brushed the debris from the cold, gray, granite marker; propping up the tiny trellis supporting the miniature rose bush, which was now full of tiny pink roses.

"You would be so proud of me, Donnie. I went to church last Sunday. Remember Sister Caroline? She moved back and had nice things to say about you...." a tear slowly rolled down Glenda's cheek.

How she missed her sweetheart. How she wished he was still with her. How she wished she had family to turn to when she needed them. Visiting Donald was a painful reminder of just how alone she was, but still she felt she needed to come.

Glenda softly continued, "I wish you were here, Donnie. I have so much I'd like to share with you. You would enjoy going through the scrapbook with me...and I'm going to go to a retreat next weekend. It would be so good to share these things with you...it would be good to share them with anyone...I mean...a person...not just Snarly...who by the way is getting really big and fat!"

The Colorado sunshine felt warm on her shoulders as she sat there twisting a blade of grass between her fingers and thumb...thinking...remembering...praying. It was quiet around her; just the faint sound of birds chirping in the distance.

A gentle breeze grazed her face. Then a soft, familiar voice whispered at the back of her neck, "Let go, Glenda...it's time to move on...its okay."

The thought sent shivers down Glenda's spine and goose bumps across her arms, but she wasn't afraid. She felt a calm sense of peace; for the first time in a very long time. She knew it was Donnie's way of telling her to move on with her life. Without warning, a large hawk landed on the stone cross just a few feet away from her. He looked intently at Glenda sitting there, tilted his head knowingly; then spread his great wings and soared away. It was the sign she had asked for.

******

At the Briarwood Nursing Home, Betty Ann waited patiently for Mark to come join her for their evening meal. He was late again. Betty Ann was getting used to the fact that her son's work often kept him from arriving promptly for the home's scheduled supper hour. But she didn't mind. She was just so thankful that she had someone who cared for her enough to make the time to be with her. There were many in the home that had no one they could rely on. Betty Ann would see them everyday. Often they would sit and stare out the window or wheel them selves up and down the hall way; searching for that once familiar face. Sometimes they just sat rubbing their heads and moaning. Betty Ann determined that being alone was what hell must be like; that total and complete separation from those who love you. What a painful existence. She remembered having a similar feeling once when she was young.

******

As the Christiansen women drove through the winding highway through the California mountains, Betty Ann felt her stomach churning. She wasn't sure if it was the winding roads or the fact that she missed her father and best friend so much. Even though she was with her sisters and mother, there was this emptiness inside of her as if she were an unfinished puzzle with a couple of pieces missing. She sniffed loudly as a gentle tear rolled down her cheek.

"What's wrong with you, Squirt?" Stella Jean whispered to her younger sister.

"Oh, nothing," Betty Ann said as she turned her head toward the side window. The sights around her were a good distraction from her thoughts of those left behind. They were coming down from the mountains and the scenery was definitely changing.

Continuing their drive toward Los Angeles, there were fewer pines and hardwood trees and more and more tall swaying palms. They drove through acres of citrus groves full of oranges, and grapefruits, and lemons.

"Oh look, Momma!" Betty Ann squealed as she pointed toward a beautiful park with flowers everywhere. "It is so beautiful...like another world!"

"That's Exposition Park, girls. Uncle Jim lives just a few miles from here. We are going to stay there for a while until we can find a place of our own to rent. Aunt June and Uncle Jim are expecting us." Mary informed her daughters while navigating through the traffic and turns to her brother's neighborhood.

"Do they have any kids?" Betty Ann asked excitedly; leaning against the seat.

Mary sighed, "No, no they don't...so they aren't used to a lot of disruption in their lives. You girls need to be on your best behavior. We are very lucky that they are willing to let us stay with them for a while until we find a place...remember that!" Mary's tone was firm.

Betty Ann sensed that this situation might be somewhat tense between her mom and uncle. "Don't worry, Momma. I'll be really good," she said softly as she leaned back in her seat. Ida Mae and Stella Jean added, "We will, too, Mom."

The Pontiac coup pulled next to the curb in front of the small brick home and Betty Ann's stomach did another flip when Uncle Jim and Aunt June appeared on the porch to greet them. They had made it to California.

******

At the Briarwood Hills Nursing Home, Mark approached his mother, seated at their table, apologetically saying, "Mom, I am so sorry for being late again. I guess you are getting used to it by now, huh?" He gave his mother a gentle kiss on the cheek.

Betty Ann smiled responding, "As l-l-long as y-y-you sh-sh-show up, I am h-h-happy."

"Oh, Mom...you know I'll always show up eventually!" Mark said laughing. "Oh, before I forget...I do need to let you know that I am going to have to be gone this coming weekend."

Betty Ann's smile left her face and suddenly she felt as if she had been punched in the stomach. Mark saw the dramatic change in his mother's expression and immediately spoke, "Mom, don't look so worried. I didn't mean to upset you. I have to speak at a seminar in Colorado...just a few days." He took his mother's hand in his and continued, "I feel I need to do this, Mom. I need to see if there is someone I might be able to help if I share my experience and knowledge with them. Please don't be upset. Aunt Stella said she wanted to come visit you from California and I thought this would be the perfect time."

At the mention of Stella's name, Betty Ann's face lit up again, "St-st-stella?" She said with excitement, "Stella is c-c-c-coming h-h-here?"

"Yes, Mom, she's coming here with her daughter, Cynthia. They are flying in on Thursday night and I am leaving that morning, so they will be coming to visit you everyday while I am gone. Do you feel better now?" Mark patted his mother's hand gently.

"Y-y-yes, th-that is w-w-w-wonderf-f-ul...th-th-thank you, M-m-mark," Betty Ann gave her son a big smile and raised his hand to her lips giving it a tender kiss.

✱✱✱✱✱✱

It had been a full day for Glenda by the time she
returned to her little house. As she approached the front
porch she could see Prince Snarls in the window, poking
his large gray striped head through the curtains, and gently
pawing at the glass as if to wave "hello". Glenda was glad
to see him and stepped up to the window gently tapping
and teasing the big cat. As she unlocked the front door she
could hear the "thud" of his pounce from the sofa to the
floor to greet her at the door.

"Hey Snarly! Boy, it's good to be home. The same
old routine at work is getting so old. I am looking forward
to going away this weekend. Are you going to be a good
boy for Father Harris when he comes to check on you?"
Glenda bent down and gently stroked the ears of the big cat
who purred gratefully. She had requested Friday off from
work for the upcoming weekend retreat. That way she
wouldn't have to rush to get there and could take her time
driving. Just the thought of going made her stomach flip
inside. She wasn't sure if it was a good feeling or a bad
one, but she was determined to go through with it and was
committed now; she had dropped the check off at the parish
on her way home from the cemetery. Father Harris was so
pleased that she decided to attend the retreat and assured
her he would pray for her while she was gone...and would
take good care of her cat.

Glenda put the copper tea kettle on the stove and
turned up the flame. She glanced at the calendar hanging on
the wall by the phone, saying, "Only two more days,
Snarly..." Her stomach did another flip, "...the day after
tomorrow...and I will be in Highland...in the mountains."

Pouring the steaming water over the aromatic tea
bag, the thought of Betty Ann's California mountain

88

experience came to her mind, "Let's check out the scrapbook, Snarly and see what our friend, Betty Ann is up to."

Sitting on the sofa and placing the warm cup of tea on the side table, she lifted the scrapbook from its place on the trunk and carefully opened it to the last page she viewed. The page was marked with the flier for the retreat she was attending in just two days. When she turned the page she noticed several photographs attached and each one had a written description under it explaining who or what was represented in the photo.

There was a picture of Betty Ann and her sisters standing in front of some dark foliage with round light fruit. "I'd say those are either very large oranges or grapefruit, Snarly. It looks like they made it through the mountains and to California." Under the picture Betty Ann had written:

Some of the delicious fruit trees close to Los Angeles.

"Look, here, Snarly...there are two new people in this picture...hmmm...it says here that the picture is of Aunt June and Uncle Jim. They must be the family they visited in California."

Glenda looked at the photos of Betty Ann and her family and wondered what that must have been like...to have people to care for you...family. She barely remembered the feeling, but longed for it again.

On the opposite page, Betty Ann had written a note and there was another picture attached at the bottom. The note read:

Uncle Jim and Aunt June don't have any children, but they knew we were coming, so Uncle Jim built this light house out of stone for us to play in. It is really tall and has steps inside that wind up to a window

at the top. Stella and Ida Mae aren't as small as me so they can't fit in it as well. I love to play in it. He also has a fish pond with real orange and white fish and Aunt June has beautiful flowers. There is a swing in the yard and they have their very own orange tree as well as an avocado tree. Those are green with bumpy peeling and soft green fruit inside that is really good with salt on it. We eat avocado sandwiches sometimes. The air here smells different. Mom says it is the salt air from the ocean. I am so excited about going to the beach. The best part about being here is that now I can write to Daddy and Margie back home in Briarwood, Nebraska and they can write back to me now, too.

At the bottom of the page was a picture of the light house with Betty Ann standing in front of it waving. Glenda rubbed the big cat's neck saying, "What a fun place to be for Betty Ann. Hey, Snarly...look it says she lived in Briarwood, Nebraska. I wonder if she still lives there...or any of her family? Why does that town sound familiar?" Betty Ann felt she had seen or heard the name of that town before. Her thoughts continued, "That might be a good clue for me to find her...I mean if she's even still alive. Gosh, I'd love to reunite her with her scrapbook if she is. I wonder how far it is to Briarwood. I'll have to check into it somehow."

Closing the book, Glenda thought about Betty Ann and her family. Even though the story wasn't about Glenda's life she somehow felt a connection to it. As she got up from the sofa and looked out the window to the darkening sky, she prayed silently. "God, if she is out there, help me find her...please." Then she went into the kitchen and prepared her evening meal for one.

10.

"Hear you're taking the day off tomorrow, Ashbury." The tall blonde hissed from her seat at the lunch table, "You got big plans or just taking some more time to *be alone*!" The other women joined her and laughed as Glenda proceeded to walked past them; on her way to the bench where she and Rose used to eat together.

Glenda paused and smiled. Taking a deep breath she, responded, "As a matter of fact, Bertha, I am going to the mountains for the weekend to meet a few friends."

It wasn't a lie, after all, she was going to the mountains and she was quite certain she would meet a few friends there. Bertha and the others were dumbfounded. They assumed Glenda had no friends, especially since Rose left, and enjoyed teasing Glenda about being a loner. But somehow it was different, now. Their words and gestures didn't bother Glenda as much. In fact, Glenda was starting to feel sorry for them...especially Bertha, who seemed to hide her insecurities behind her bullying and hurtful remarks. As Glenda took her place on the bench, she glanced up from her lunch and noticed Bertha staring at her. Glenda smiled and waved. Bertha quickly turned away in shame.

*****

The woman carefully steered her motorized wheelchair down the long hallway at the Brairwood Hills Nursing Home, but paused suddenly at Betty Ann's doorway. Betty Ann was seated near the window, diligently painting; facing her easel with her back to the door.

"That is a lovely painting." The woman said as she waited just outside the doorway, "Mind if I come in and get a closer look?"

Betty Ann turned her wheelchair so she could see who was speaking to her. She had seen this woman several times in the activities groups and they had occasionally been in physical therapy at the same time. She was slightly younger than Betty Ann with beautiful dark brown skin and black hair with silver streaks, which curled softly around her face. She wore braces on both arms and was missing both legs; just below the knees.

Betty Ann responded, "W-w-well, it's f-f-far from f-f-finished, b-b-but if you w-w-want to c-c-come in, y-y-you are w-w-welcomed t-to d-do so."

The woman eagerly entered the room, expertly guiding her chair through the narrow passages between the bed and dresser to the open area by the window. "The colors are so beautiful...and the waves look so real crashing against the rocks like that. Look how when the sun shines on them they look almost transparent. It looks like a great place to visit...did you go there once?"

Betty Ann smiled. "Y-Y-Yes, a v-v-very l-long t-time a-g-go, w-when I w-was y-y-young." She said as she placed the brush down on the palette on her lap. She turned her chair to face the woman. Reaching her hand out, she spoke slowly, "M-m-y n-n-name is B-b-betty Ann. How l-long have y-you l-lived here?"

The woman allowed Betty Ann to shake her hand and sighed, "Too long," then laughed, adding, "But it is a hundred times better than some of the other places I was in while I lived in the city. The small town nursing homes are much nicer than the big city ones. Everyone here seems to really care about you...and the food is much better, too. It feels more like family here, I guess. Oh, my name is Laura."

"D-d-do you h-h-have a f-f-family, L-L-Laura?" Betty Ann asked the woman; wondering why she was in the care of the nursing home rather than with them.

"I did have. They were killed in the same accident that did this to me," she said as she clumsily patted her stumps of legs with her brace supported hands, "It was many years ago and I've been living in places like this ever since...but this has been the best and hopefully...probably my last."

"I-I-I'm s-s-so s-s-sorry. It m-m-must be hard t-t-to b-b-be alone l-l-like this." Betty Ann wished her speech was smoother, but Laura didn't seem to mind.

Many times she could see the pain of anxiousness on the faces of those she spoke with. They would lean toward her as she spoke as if to try and encourage each word to flow smoothly from her lips. Laura's face was warm and friendly and there was a twinkle in her hazel brown eyes. Betty Ann was just thankful for the ability to communicate once again; broken as it was.

Laura sighed and smiled, "You know, at first I was just so angry and mean. That's why I ended up in so many different places. It was ugly. I just couldn't understand why God would take away my husband and sister like that...they were all I had left. My parents both died years before. It took many years of therapy and a great deal of prayer to get me through it. I had to learn to stop blaming God and start thanking Him for being alive. What about you? I see that nice young man who comes to join you for supper every night. Is he your son?"

"Yes, th-that's M-Mark. He is s-s-so g-g-good to m-m-me." Betty Ann was pleased that Laura could see the kindness in her son. "I h-h-have a s-s-sist-t-ter, too. Sh-she l-l-lives in Cal-lif-f-fornia." Although Betty Ann was enjoying the company, the effort to converse was fatiguing her. She took a slow deep breath and smiled. She wanted to add that her other sister, Ida Mae, had died a few years back, but she was getting too tired to discuss it.

"California, huh? That would explain the picture you are painting of the ocean. I bet it is a beautiful place. I've never been there, but looking at this painting makes me feel like I have," Laura said as she studied the painting.

"Th-th-thank y-y-you, L-L-Laura. Wh-when it is f-f-f-fin-n-nished I w-w-will g-g-give it to y-y-you." Betty Ann said, smiling. She loved to give her paintings away to those who appreciated them.

"Really? Oh that would be wonderful! I would love it. I guess I should go then so you can finish it," Laura said as she winked at Betty Ann, adding "You're a really talented lady, Betty Ann. I hope we can talk again, soon. Thanks, again." Laura backed her chair out of the room.

"Y-you're w-w-wel-come. Th-th-thanks f-f-for st-st-stopping by," Betty Ann waved as Laura left her room. Then she thought to herself, "I am so tired. Talking just wears me out, but I know I must practice it in order to get better again. The therapist says I've come a long way in a short time." She turned to look at the painting remembering how the sound of the waves and the smell of the ocean once filled air surrounding her.

When Glenda returned home that day she held Prince Snarls in her arms. The cat purred as his mistress stroked his back and said, "It will be good to get away this weekend, even though I will miss you, Snarly. I'm especially looking forward to a reprieve from work and that big mouth, Bertha. She just isn't a very nice person, Snarly, but then, I guess, that's what makes this world interesting...all the different people who live in it. Think how boring it would be if we all thought alike and acted alike." Prince Snarls had enough attention and wiggled free of Glenda's arms. He took his place on the back of the sofa and immediately began his nightly ritual of grooming.

Glenda reached for the scrapbook and turned the pages; reflecting on all she had learned about Betty Ann and her family. Turning past the page with the photo of the stone lighthouse, there was a yellowed, aged envelope glued to the following page. Glenda gently lifted the flap of the envelope to reveal the bulging contents. Inside was sand, contained in tissue paper. "Betty Ann must have made it to the beach to see the ocean," Glenda said to herself as she felt the gritty sand between her fingers and thumb.

There were photographs of Betty Ann and Stella Jean posing on the beach in various acrobatic positions. In one photo Stella Jean was smiling effortlessly while doing the splits between two elevated boxes; a view of the ocean behind her. There were photos of Ida Mae and Mary wading in the water with their pant legs rolled up. On the next two pages, Betty Ann had created drawings of sea gulls soaring, starfish, and various styles and shapes of boats on the water.

There was one remarkable photo that caught Glenda's attention. It was a close-up of Betty Ann. The ocean breeze was blowing through her curly hair as she looked directly at the photographer; smiling. Glenda looked into the light colored eyes, which seemed to peer deep into her soul, and said, "Where are you Betty Ann? Are you still alive? How can I find you?"

✲✲✲✲✲✲

The nurse aide assisted Betty Ann in transferring from her wheel chair to the bed, and glanced at the beautiful painting of the ocean on the easel by the window. The gentle glow of the dim light above the bed seemed to make the picture come to life; as if she could hear the squawk of the sea gulls soaring in the sky and the roar of the waves against the shore. She turned to Betty Ann and said softly, "You are one talented lady."

Betty Ann smiled and replied, "G-G-God has g-g-g-given m-me m-m-m-many b-b-blessings."

The aide paused at the door, saying, "Good night Betty Ann...Sweet dreams."

Betty Ann gently folded her hands across her breast as she prepared to participate in her nightly ritual of talking to God; praising Him for all her many blessings and asking His protection on her loved ones as they travel. Tomorrow she will see her sister, Stella Jean and Mark will be on his way to Colorado.

11.

It was cloudy and looked like rain that early Friday morning when Father Harris came to Glenda's house to meet Prince Snarls and discuss his care. Glenda had barely slept a wink and was nervously anticipating her weekend retreat at the Highland Monastery. She had her bags packed and waiting at the door. Prince Snarls had watched her curiously as she put each item in the suitcase. He paced around the bags, sniffing them cautiously, but when the doorbell rang he leaped to the sofa and peaked through the sheer curtain at the figure waiting on the porch. His tail began to swish back and forth in anticipation.

"Good morning, Father," Glenda greeted the priest as she invited him in, "It looks like it wants to rain on us today."

"I'm afraid so, Glenda. Maybe it will just be a gentle rain and not like the one we had last weekend. That was quite a storm." Father Harris stood on the rug just inside the door, Glancing at the suitcases sitting by the door he said, "It looks like you are ready to go."

"Well, I don't know about ready...but I'm packed anyway," Glenda responded. She hadn't been away from her home in many years, and she had never left Snarly...ever. Even though she was anticipating the adventure she felt guilty as she glanced over at the big cat now crouched in the corner of the sofa; ears flat against his head, tail swishing nervously and eyes widely fixed on Father Harris.

"I think your cat is a little upset over this," Father Harris stated as he cautiously sat down on the sofa next to the big gray striped cat. Prince Snarls slowly released an eerie moan and backed into the arm of the sofa. Father Harris gently laid his hand, palm side up, on the sofa between himself and Snarly, saying, "Its okay, boy...I'm a friend. You don't have to be afraid."

97

Snarly fixed his eyes on the priest and cautiously approached the open hand presented before him. As the cat sniffed Father Harris' hand his ears relaxed and his tail stopped the nervous swishing. Snarly then rubbed his face into the palm of the priest's hand and purred. Father Harris gently rolled his hand over to caress the ears of the big cat. They had become friends.

Glenda laughed with amazement, "Wow, Father...that was pretty neat. I wasn't sure if he would accept you or not. I feel much better about leaving now." She showed Father Harris where all the necessities were for Prince Snarls; especially the drawer containing his favorite treats. She cautioned, "It would probably be best not to let Snarly go outside at all while I am gone. Since this is the first time I have ever left him, I'm afraid of what he would do. He may not come back in for you."

The big cat was now happily purring on Father Harris' lap. "We'll be fine, Glenda. I won't let him go out and I'll sit with him when I visit so he will have some companionship. Don't worry about him. Just relax and rejuvenate yourself at the retreat. I will pray that you will feel especially close to God this weekend and gain a better understanding of his plan for your life. In fact I will stay a bit after you leave so Snarly doesn't feel everyone is leaving him at the same time, if you'd like. Oh...do you need help with those?" Father Harris said pointing to the bags by the door.

Glenda was impressed with Father Harris' understanding of animals. "You be a good boy for Father." she said, and added, "The bags are small, Father. I think I can manage them." She put one over her shoulder and pulled out the handle on the other, rolling it through the door.

Glenda felt comfortable leaving Snarly in Father Harris' care. Loading the bags into her little car, she noticed Prince Snarls sitting on the back of the sofa peeking through the curtains as Father Harris waved.

The rain was beating steadily on the windshield of the little Volkswagen Beetle as the rhythm of the wipers was faintly heard behind the stereo while the Beatles sang "Hey Jude". Glenda hadn't listened to that CD for sometime. She remembered how she had shared with Rose her "Hey Jude ritual", and wondered where Rose was now...since her family's deportation. Glenda turned off the CD.

The sky was beginning to clear as Glenda approached the mountain village of Highland. It was a quaint little village with whimsical shops along the main street and a wooden covered bridge which carried traffic across the babbling Elk Creek that wound its way through town. When the sun broke through the clouds, Glenda lowered the side window allowing the fresh mountain air in. The scent of the pines, warmed by the sun filled the air and she enjoyed the flicker of the bright green aspen leaves as they caught the sun's rays with the breeze. It had been a long time since she had seen the beauty of the mountains.

The Volkswagen easily maneuvered the hair-pin curves leading up to the Highland Monastery. But Glenda didn't push the little car and allowed the other vehicles to pass her along the way; sometimes pulling over on the shoulder to let them go by. She was enjoying the beauty around her so much that she drove right past the obscure entrance of the Monastery; catching just a glimpse of the log pine sign as she drove by. She quickly pulled off onto the shoulder and stopped. Since she was only a few feet beyond the entrance, she cautiously backed the little car down the road to the entrance and turned onto the road under the pine log sign which read:

Highland Monastery

The road leading to the monastery was shrouded with tall pines and aspens that blocked out the sky. Occasionally the suns rays could be seen through the openings of the branches. There were beautiful blue Columbine and pale pink wild roses scattered along the roadside. Suddenly, the woods opened to a clearing with a large log building perched on the mountainside; along with several smaller buildings of the same design.

Glenda parked her car in the visitors' parking lot just below a beautiful garden area; meticulously and ritualistically maintained by the nuns at the monastery. As Glenda struggled to pull the bag from the back seat of her car, she was startled by a voice behind her.

"Can I help you with that?" Glenda turned suddenly, and losing her balance, felt a strong hand on her arm helping her regain her stance.
Looking up, her eyes were met by the most beautiful blue eyes she had ever seen. They looked deep into her soul and there was something vaguely familiar about them. Embarrassed by her clumsiness, Glenda turned away; focusing her attention on removing the suitcase.

As the bag finally released, Glenda turned to the man and smiled, saying, "Uh...thanks. But I think I've got in now."

Regaining her balance, she leaned on the willow cane and pulled the retractable handle from the suitcase. The man gently released his grasp on Glenda's arm and closed the car door as she stepped away from him. "I'm fine...really...thanks," Glenda said firmly, avoiding those piercing eyes.

"Okay, okay...just thought you could use a little help, that's all. You sure you can get everything all right? I could help you, you know. I think we're headed to the same place." He bent down trying to make eye contact with the little red-head.

Glenda could feel her cheeks getting warm and knew she was blushing. Cautiously she raised her eyes, hoping he had turned away, but once again his eyes caught hers and held them like a magnet on metal.

The handsome man smiled and held out his hand, "My name is Mark...Mark Bryant. What's your name?"

Glenda slowly offered her right hand, saying, "Glenda...I'm Glenda Ashbury. I guess I could use the help, Mark...thanks."

Mark picked up the carry-on bag. Putting the strap over his shoulder he carefully took the handle of the other suitcase from Glenda's hand. At first Glenda clutched the handle firmly in protest, but Mark smiled tenderly saying gently, "Let me, Glenda...its okay." And so they walked up the long path, through the garden and approached the large wooden doors of the monastery. Mark walked slowly allowing Glenda time to balance her steps against the willow cane.

Neither of them spoke until they reached the lobby of the monastery when Glenda turned to Mark and said, "Thanks, Mark for the helping hand. That was very kind of you."

Mark placed the handle of the roller bag in Glenda's hand and carefully placed the shoulder strap of the smaller bag over Glenda's shoulder; gently lifting her shoulder length red curls out from under the strap and, purposefully, allowing his hand to tenderly brush the side of her neck. His touch sent shivers down Glenda's spine and once again she felt the warmth of a blush across her cheeks.

Mark smiled and winked, "Have a great time at the retreat, Glenda Ashbury. Maybe I'll see you around." As Mark walked down the long hallway, Glenda watched him carefully, until he turned left at the end of the hall and out of sight.

Approaching the registration table, Glenda found her name tag and welcome packet. A smiling woman, waiting at the end of the table, greeted her saying, "Welcome, Glenda Ashbury. I trust your stay at Highland Monastery will be a memorable one. We here at the monastery love to share our home with others as they learn and grow with God. My name is Sister Joan, and I will be the one you can come to if you need anything special. You will be on the second floor. Let's take the elevator, okay?"

The elevator doors opened on the second floor and Glenda and Sister Joan turned to the right down a long hall modestly decorated with a few small tables displaying the fresh flowers from the garden. There was a crucifix at the end of the hall. On the right side of the hall was a door with a small sign to the side which read, *Pod B.* There were four name slots beneath the sign. Sister Joan slid Glenda's name into a slot. This would be her place of residency for the next few days.

"There's a bathroom just up the hall across from the elevator with showers for your use. We only ask one thing..." Sister Joan looked very serious, continuing, "...please do not flush the toilets with your foot. It weakens the handles!" Then she laughed. "Ah, here's your bunk," she said pausing at the end of the divided sleeping areas. "You are blessed to have a window to look out."

The nun continued to show Glenda where she could hang her clothes and which dresser drawers where hers to use as the dresser was shared by the person in the bunk across from her. Turning to Glenda, she took her hands and said, "Dinner is served at six o'clock. Your time is yours for now."

Glenda thanked Sister Joan and started putting away her things. Gradually, other women arrived on the second floor, but the bunk across from Glenda's still hadn't been claimed. Glenda was actually hoping no one would take it. She liked her isolation as it felt familiar and comfortable.

Dinner was served, buffet style, in a very large cafeteria. The room was full of men and women; many who knew and greeted each other warmly. Glenda didn't recognize anyone at first, but then she noticed Mark sitting across the room with a group of people who were obviously very comfortable with each other. Their laughter carried throughout the dining hall. Glenda lifted the food tray carefully with her right hand and grasping her cane in her left walked to the nearest table to sit. Looking up, she realized she had a perfect view of Mark and he was looking at her; smiling and waving. Glenda smiled and then looked away; trying hard not to notice his eyes on her.

******

"Betty! Betty Ann...It's you...it really is you!" Stella Jean exclaimed, tearfully, as she carefully bent over her walker to give her sister a hug. "It is so good to finally see you again. You look beautiful, dear, and I hear you are getting the ol' fire back again." The same twinkle sparked in her eyes as she held her little sister's face in her hand and kissed her cheek.

"St-St-Stella! I am s-s-s-s-so glad t-t-t-to s-see you! D-d-d-don't l-l-let th-this ch-ch-ch-chair f-f-fool y-y-you! I'm st-st-still k-k-kicking!" Betty Ann smiled a huge smile and squeezed her sister's hand. "H-H-How w-w-was your f-f-flight?"

"Oh it was great, Aunt Betty," Cynthia answered as she bent down to give her aunt a kiss. "Mom got a window seat and enjoyed the view. Mark told us that your rehab was going well, but I am impressed with how well you really are doing. I'm so happy for you."

"It's b-b-been a l-l-little t-t-tough, b-b-but I'm d-d-determined!" Betty Ann smiled.

Stella sat on the winged chair in the family meeting room, "You were always able to do anything you put your mind to, dear," she said as she held Betty Ann's hand in hers. "You were always the optimistic one in the family."

"And y-y-you w-w-were the o-o-one w-w-with th-the b-b-best f-f-flexib-b-bility!" Betty Ann said laughing. "Rem-m-memb-b-ber th-those d-d-days?" She added, patting her sister's hand.

"Mother and I were just talking about that on the plane, Aunt Betty. She loves to tell the story of the time you went to California during the depression to earn money. She said you kept a scrapbook of the whole adventure. Do you still have it?" Cynthia asked as she removed the light jacket from her mother's shoulders and set the walker to the side of the chair.

"N-n-no, D-d-d-dear. It w-w-w-was l-l-lost...y-y-years ago. I th-th-th-think it w-w-was l-left in a b-b-box in a m-moving v-van. It w-w-was wh-when Uncle T-T-Tim and I m-m-moved b-b-back f-from Color-rado...m-m-many y-years ago...b-before M-Mark w-was even b-b-born. Uncle T-T-Tim w-was s-s-stationed th-th-there f-for a t-t-time," Betty Ann took a deep breath and let it out slowly. Conversation was still a challenge for her.

"Gee, Aunt Betty, that's too bad. I bet there was a lot of neat stuff in that old scrapbook. I would have loved to have seen it. Mom tells the stories and I imagine them in my mind, but it would be awesome to have the pictures and a written record of it all. You girls were really something...you still are," Cynthia said, hugging her mom and aunt. "Would you like some coffee? I know I could use a cup. Oh, look, Mom, they have a soft serve machine. Aunt Betty, would you like me to put some vanilla ice cream in your coffee? It's really yummy that way. Mom and I have it that way at Ocean View Assisted Living."

"Th-that s-s-sounds l-like a g-g-good t-treat, Cindy, d-d-dear. Th-th-thank y-you," Betty liked the idea of the cool ice cream in the warm coffee. "Sh-she's a s-sweet g-girl, S-Stella." Betty Ann knew Cynthia had gone through a rough time in high school, but was glad to see her so grown up.

"I am so fortunate to have her close by," Stella stated. "And you have Mark. How is he doing these days? Does he have anyone special in his life?"

"Other th-than m-m-me?" Betty laughed, "N-n-no, not y-yet. He w-w-works s-s-so hard and I w-w-wish he w-w-would t-t-take th-the t-t-time to d-d-date m-m-more. I j-j-just w-want t-to get b-b-better s-s-so he c-c-can."

When Cynthia brought the special coffees to the women, she sat back and listened to them share the stories of their days living in California. She offered tissues as they spoke of their sister, Ida Mae; referring to her as "the glue that held them all together" and the selfless love of their mother. Both women agreed the experience they had of going to school and performing in California helped them to become more accepting towards people who were of a greater variety than those living in Briarwood, Nebraska. Cynthia realized that in front of her was a legacy that was worth remembering and she just sat back and listened to the many stories that started with "Remember when...." and allowed her imagination to take her back.

******

The Christiansen women finally saved up enough money to move into a tiny one room flat of their own. It was located above a small, but very busy, bakery and just a couple blocks from the beautiful Exposition Park where Stella and Betty did their practicing. They couldn't afford much and the room only had one bed which Mary and

Stella Jean slept in at night and Ida Mae slept in during the day. Betty Ann's bed was on top of an old trunk (at least it had a flat top) and fit her fine since she was so small. Ida Mae had found a job working nights as a car hop in one of the many drive-in food restaurants, which were so popular. Mary helped out in the bakery downstairs during the day while Stella Jean and Betty Ann went to school.

Betty Ann loved living in the city and especially so close to such a beautiful park. It was a great place to just run around and meet other kids. The girls could take a street car for a dime and get transfers to just about anywhere. There were movie theaters and talent contests going on all the time. But the best part was school.

The class room was brightly decorated with the student's art work and writings. Sitting at their desks were children of all shades of skin and hair color. As Betty Ann stood at the front of the class with Miss Barkley's hand on her shoulder, she looked around the room. All she could think of was her favorite Sunday school song which she had learned in church back in Briarwood:

"Jesus loves the little children...all little children of the world...red and yellow black and white...they are precious in his sight...Jesus loves the little children of the world."

Miss Barkley cleared her throat and said, "Class we have a new student joining us all the way from Nebraska. Her name is Betty Ann Christiansen. Please be sure to give her a warm California greeting. Betty Ann, there is a desk for you over there, next to Martha." Miss Barkley directed her attention to the second row and third desk back. Across from the empty desk was a young girl with dark skin and black hair which had several braids secured with bright ribbons to match her pretty plaid dress. As Glenda

106

approached the desk, the girl smiled, revealing the prettiest and whitest teeth Glenda had ever seen.

"Hi! My name is Martha Jones. I'm glad to meet you, Glenda. I hope you will like living in California." The young girl reached out and shook Glenda's hand.

In front of Glenda was a boy with hair as dark as Martha, only straight, and his skin was very light. His eyes were like narrow slits in his face. He was oriental...maybe Chinese or Japanese, Glenda thought. Across from her was a girl with a beautiful red dress trimmed in white lace. She had long, wavy, brown hair and dark brown eyes and her skin was the color of coffee with cream. She smiled shyly at Glenda and waved. All around her were children of various race and ethnic backgrounds. There was nothing like this in Briarwood. Somehow, it just made the big world seem a little smaller. She was going to like it here.

Suddenly she felt a sharp poke in her back. "Ouch!" Glenda said, turning to face a rather chubby boy with red hair and freckles. "What'd you go and poke me for?" She asked sternly.

The boy leaned over the top of his desk and whispered, "I hear they got cowboys and Indians back in Nebraska? Is that why you left there?"

Betty Ann couldn't believe what she was hearing, so she decided to have a little fun and replied, "Yeah, they are always fighting and we just got tired of all the shooting and scalping and stuff." The boy's eyes grew wide and he just leaned back in his seat. Betty Ann looked over at Martha and winked. Martha covered her mouth and giggled.

******

Father Harris shut off the light to his office and closed the door. It was time for him to go to Glenda's and feed Prince Snarls. As he walked out the large wooden doors exiting the rectory, his thoughts went to Glenda and he said a quick prayer for God to draw near to her while she was on her retreat.

Prince Snarls was watching at the window as Father Harris approached the front door. When the priest opened the door he heard the "thump" of the big cat as he jumped down from the back of the sofa.

"Hey, there, Snarly. How are you today?" Father Harris said as he bent down to rub the cat's arched back, "You ready to eat?"

Prince Snarls wove in and out of the priest's legs, meowing softly as Father Harris dumped the dry cat food into one dish and put fresh water in the other. "Here you go, Snarly." He set the dishes on the floor and Prince Snarls sniffed them but sat and looked up at the priest tilting his head. "I believe you want me to just sit and pet you for a bit before you eat." Father Harris commented as he sat down on the sofa in Glenda's living room. The big cat jumped up on the sofa and rubbed up against the priest's large belly begging for attention. "Okay, okay...I'll stay for a bit," he said, rubbing the big cat's ears.

As they sat together on the sofa, Father Harris noticed the scrapbook on the trunk in front of them. "What's this?" He said leaning forward to pick it up. "I'm sure Glenda wouldn't mind if I take a look,"

He carefully turned the pages of the book, skimming through the first pages of Betty Ann and her family. Suddenly, there was something very familiar on the page in front of him. He had turned just past the page that Glenda had marked and recognized the pictures Betty Ann had drawn of the ocean; having been born and raised in California himself. Looking at them brought back wonderful memories of playing at the beach and the fun gatherings with his childhood friends at beautiful Exposition Park.

On the next page was a letter which he chose not to read but the following page there was an old class picture. He couldn't believe his eyes. Could it be? But how could it? He drew the book and photo closer. It was! It was his class picture from Los Angeles, California. There in front of him, was Miss Barkley and sitting cross-legged, on the ground, in the front row, was a little chubby light haired boy with freckles. A boy he knew well. A boy who thought he'd move to Nebraska to fight with the cowboys and Indians...but became a priest in Colorado instead.

"Well, I'll be..." Father Harris commented as he set the scrapbook back down on the trunk. "I wonder how this scrapbook relates to Glenda and her life. That was such and interesting year for our class. I remember there was this new girl who came...what was her name? Betty...Betty Ann Christiansen...I think...that's right. She was an acrobat or something. Oh my goodness! Could it be? Could this scrapbook belong to the same Betty Ann that I knew? That little red haired girl from Nebraska who spent more time walking on her hands than on her feet? And how does Glenda know her? This is something I will have to ask Glenda about when she gets back." He carefully closed the scrapbook and placed it back on the trunk. Getting up from the sofa, he turned to Snarly who was already positioned on the back of the sofa, and said, "Well, Snarly, time for me to go. I will see you tomorrow."

******

After dinner Glenda and the others were directed to a large meeting room where there were round tables set up with notebooks and pens at each place setting. The first speaker for the night was preparing in one of the other rooms and there was an elderly nun skillfully playing the piano at the front of the room.

Glenda found an empty chair at the nearest table by the door and took her seat. Men and women were trickling in through the three entrances into the room. Someone stepped up to the microphone and spoke, "Testing, testing...one...two...three..." Another person at the far end of the room gave a thumbs up signal and the two exited out the side door.

"Mind if I join you?" The familiar voice sounded from behind Glenda.

"Sure, Sister...I mean...that would be fine, "Glenda said, turning around, adding, "It looks like the place is filling up fast."

"Oh, there's a seat for everyone registered," Sister Joan responded, "These speakers are usually quite enjoyable. I hear this one came from a little town in Nebraska and has a wonderful sense of humor." As she opened the notebook on the table in front of her she told Glenda, "You can write your name on your notebook. It's yours to keep for the duration of the retreat...just in case you want to take notes."

Glenda opened the small notebook and wrote her name on the inside cover. At the top of the first page she wrote: My retreat - Day One. Glancing around the room, she noticed the tables were now filled. There was a buzz of conversation in the air and she thought, "Hmmm...I don't see Mark anywhere. Maybe he decided to skip this meeting."

"What's wrong, Glenda?" Sister Joan asked, observing the searching expression on Glenda's face as she scanned the crowd, "You look like you're missing someone."

Glenda could feel the warmth of a blush flowing into her cheeks and she quickly responded, "Me? Oh, no...no...I'm not missing anyone. I mean...I don't even know anyone here to miss...not really."

Sister Joan smiled and patted Glenda's hand, whispering, "Well, don't worry, dear, you'll meet plenty of people soon. Just look around this table. Here are eight other new possibilities for friendship," she said, smiling at the others sitting around them. "All you have to do is be open to the opportunity."

A sudden hush came over the crowd as a priest stepped up to the microphone, saying, "Good evening ladies and gentlemen...and Sisters. My name is Father Joseph and I am the priest in Moosetown...just north of here a few miles. It is so good to see all of you here. Tonight we have a very special speaker who comes to us from our neighboring state of Nebraska. Please join me in welcoming, Mr. Mark Bryant."

The crowd burst into applause and Glenda's mouth dropped open. Mark bounced up the steps to the platform and reaching the stage, did a full cart-wheel; landing right in front of the podium and microphone. His antics brought roars of laughter and cheers from the crowd. Mark's eyes twinkled and his smile was contagious. Smoothing out his hair and catching his breath he bent toward the microphone, and said, "Good evening, everyone! That's just one of the many wonderful things my mother taught me. She always said it was a good attention grabber!"

Again, the crowd laughed and applauded. Glenda was stunned. Her heart was racing and she felt as if she was under water; unable to catch her breath. She could see Mark talking, but only seemed to hear bits and pieces of his presentation. At one point, he spotted Glenda in the crowd and winked at her while smoothly continuing his talk on life's possibilities and healing with laughter. He was a natural speaker and the crowd loved him. Glenda was secretly growing fond of him, too.

Sister Joan noticed the subtle interaction between Mark and Glenda. Leaning toward Glenda she whispered, "I thought you said you didn't know anyone here."

Glenda could feel her cheeks flush again and responded, smiling, "I didn't think I did."

12.

"Rise and shine!" Sister Joan called out as she knocked on the doors leading to each sleeping area on the second floor. Glenda glanced at her watch on the small table next to her bed and moaned, "Five thirty a.m.! You've got to be kidding!"

"She's not kidding!" a voice responded from the bunk across the narrow hall, "I've been here before and this is the usual routine."

Glenda sat up in her bunk and pulled back the privacy curtain that surrounded her sleeping space, commenting, "Sounds like I finally got a neighbor."

As Glenda's new neighbor struggled to pull back her privacy curtain she laughed, "Yeah, I arrived late last night. My name is Polly Petersen. I guess I missed the first speaker. Was he any good?"

Glenda smiled as she remembered Mark's pre-speech ice breaker and her heart flipped at the memory of his wink directed her way. She looked at Polly and said, "Yeah, he was very entertaining and his talk was inspirational. It was about healing with laughter and appreciating life's possibilities. He did a cart-wheel on the stage! Oh, my name is Glenda...Glenda Ashbury."

"He did what?" Polly said as she flopped down on her pillow at the foot of her bed.

"A cart-wheel," Glenda continued, "you know...feet over head. It was pretty funny. He said it was just one of the many things he learned from his mother!"

Polly was laughing, "What a riot! I wonder if he'll speak again. I'm sorry I missed it. Hey, was he cute?"

Glenda was making her bed and stopped suddenly, "Cute? Uh...well...I don't know. I...uh...guess you could say so," adding quickly, "I didn't really notice." She could feel a flush come over her cheeks and turned her back to Polly so she wouldn't notice.

"So, do you think he'll speak again? I hope so. I could use a little humor in my life." Polly grabbed her towel and toothbrush, saying, "Well, I'm gonna' go do my morning thing...so I'll catch up with you later, Glenda."

Glenda waved and smiled responding, "Remember...don't use your foot to flush the toilet!" She could hear Polly laughing as she walked down the hall.

Glenda gazed out the window and observed the distant snow topped peaks of the Rocky Mountains catching the glow of the pale pink light of the morning sunrise. She could see the beautiful garden below. Opening the window, the soothing sound of the cascading water from Elk Creek could be heard as it tumbled over the rocks. The early morning mountain air was crisp and cool and filled with the aroma of pine.

In the garden below, well groomed pathways radiated out from a central cobblestone hub and there were strategically placed benches facing beautiful displays of flowers, greenery, and statues of angels and saints. At the center of the hub, where all the paths came together, was a large glistening fountain. Glenda decided she would go for a walk in the garden later that morning during her reflection time.

Glenda picked up her small flowered travel bag, containing her morning personal needs, and a clean white towel, which was neatly folded on the small shelf of her closet space. She slipped on her red flip-flops and grasped her willow cane to proceed toward the bathroom down the hall.

Polly was approaching her and exclaimed, "It's all yours...well, yours and about five others!" Turning and walking backwards, she added, "Hey, I'll meet you down stairs. We can sit together at breakfast, if you'd like."

Glenda admired Polly's agility as she leaned against her willow cane with each step. She remembered when she was just as light on her feet. She smiled and sighed, responding, "Sounds good. I'll see you downstairs...save me a seat!" Polly gave a thumbs-up and turned to walk back to their sleeping pod to get dressed for the day.

******

At the Brairwood Hills Nursing Home, Miss Swanson passed by the dining table and said, "Good morning, Betty Ann. Are you going with us to spend some time in the garden today?"

It was time for the weekly group outing. Briarwood had a wonderful flower garden which was established by a prominent family and maintained by volunteers. Betty Ann was one of those volunteers before she became ill. How she loved planting the flowers in the spring and tending to them throughout the year. She didn't even mind the hours of weeding that were needed in order to keep the display as beautiful as possible. Working in the garden reminded her of living in California near the beautiful Exposition Park.

"I am l-l-looking f-forward to g-going t-t-to the g-g-garden," Betty Ann replied to Miss Swanson, as she stood by her table, "It l-looks like a b-beautiful d-day outside."

"It is a beautiful day. I think it will be good for all of us to get some sunshine. We'll be going out after lunch. Would your sister and niece like to join us?" Miss Swanson asked, bending down toward Betty Ann.

"I b-believe they would, th-thank you." Betty Ann replied, smiling.

"See you then," Miss Swanson stated as she walked away from the dining area and toward the hall.

About an hour later, Miss Swanson knocked on the door frame to Betty Ann's room. She had an envelope in her hands, and stated, "I'm sorry, I forgot to give this to you when I saw you earlier." She handed Betty Ann the light pink envelope.

Looking at the envelope, Betty Ann recognized the handwriting and carefully lifted the flap which was secured by a silver embossed seal with the raised letter **B** on it. It was a card from Mark; just to let her know he was thinking of her while he was gone. "He must have mailed this the day he left," Betty Ann thought. She turned to look at the picture of Mark and her proudly displayed on the dresser. It was taken before her stroke and he was standing behind her with his arms affectionately wrapped around her shoulders. Next to that photograph was a picture of Betty Ann and Tim on their honeymoon. They had spent a week at the lake and were sitting together in a wooden boat. Tim's arms were wrapped around Betty Ann's shoulders in the same manner as Mark's were in the other photo, but Tim had his face pressed close to Betty Ann's lovingly. There was a third picture, yellowed with age and in an oval frame. In this picture Betty Ann was being held protectively in the arms of John Christiansen, her father. It was taken the day she arrived home from California.

Admiring the photos of the three men in her life, Betty Ann noticed the many similarities in their features; the same strong, square jaws and those beautiful penetrating eyes. How happy these men had made her. How blessed she was to have been a part of their lives. Looking down at the beautiful card in her hands and reading the sweet sentiment one more time, she was thankful to know that someone was thinking of her and took the time to let her know. Gazing out to the sunny Nebraska morning, she remembered this feeling from another time in her past.

******

     Mary Christiansen carefully tore open the envelope with the familiar return address in the upper left corner. The envelope was addressed to "Mary Christiansen and daughters" and was from John, back in Briarwood. How thankful she was they were able to correspond again.

     "Is it a letter from Daddy?" Betty Ann asked, excitedly. "How is he? How are things back home? Does he say anything about anybody else?" Even though California provided many new adventures and opportunities, Betty Ann missed her life in Briarwood, Nebraska. She missed her father and her best friend, Margie. She often wondered if Margie's brother, Tim, even noticed she was gone.

     "Hold on, Betty Ann...I haven't even read the letter myself yet. Let's see...sounds like things are getting better back home. Dad says he's been busy at the shop finally. With all the new government programs for work, people have money to spend again. He says he really misses us all and he has been busy trying to fix up the house for our return. The couple who are renting the house gave Dad the back room to sleep in when the weather turned so cold. They will be moving out in the spring because the man accepted a job in the city. Dad says he wants to paint the walls inside the house so everything will be like new when we come home."

     Mary's eyes filled with tears as she silently read the last few lines from John. He was telling her how much he loved her and missed her and how sorry he was that he was not able to provide better for them. She took a deep breath and then smiled at her daughters, saying, "Maybe we'll be able to go home soon...we'll see." Reaching in her apron pocket, she said, "Oh, Betty Ann, there's a letter for you here, too." Mary handed the envelope to her daughter.

"It's from Margie!" Betty Ann squealed with delight. She quickly tore open the envelope and flopped down across the bed and read the following:

Dear Betty Ann,

How are you? I am fine. So, what have you been doing lately? What is it like in California? It is so cold here. Is it hot there? It snowed again yesterday. Tim and I went sledding with some of the other kids in the neighborhood. Speaking of Tim, he asked me if I heard from you lately. I don't know why he would care.

Well, that is about all for now. Write to me when you get the chance. I miss you!
Your Best Friend,
Margie Bryant
P.S. I still have my necklace. Do you still have yours?

Betty Ann touched the half heart charm around her neck and smiled. She gave a big sigh as she read the part about Tim asking about her and thought silently, "Tim asked about me!" Maybe he was missing her, too. She liked to daydream about him and often imagined them getting married someday. She carefully folded the letter and put it back in the envelope; tucking it away safely between the pages of her scrapbook.

Glenda and Polly were enjoying their breakfasts in the large dining hall when Sister Joan stepped up behind Glenda and gently touched Glenda's shoulder. Leaning forward, she placed a small white envelope on the table.

"I was asked to deliver this to you Glenda," she said, "if you need to reply, you can give the message to me and I will deliver it. This is our internet system here at the Monastery...pretty unique, huh?" Sister Joan chuckled as she walked away.

Polly took a sip of her coffee and said, "So, you have a special delivery message! Aren't you going to open it and see what it is?"

Glenda just stared at the envelope on the table in front of her. Who would be writing to her here? Maybe it was an encouraging note from Father Harris? She carefully picked up the envelope and gently lifted the flap which was secured by an embossed foil sticker with a raised letter *B* on it. When she opened the card, her eyes immediately went to the signature at the bottom of the note, Mark Bryant. Glenda's heart skipped a beat and she could feel her face flush as she read the message in the card,

Dear Glenda,
Please meet me by the fountain in the garden
today at 11:00am.
I would like to talk with you.
Mark Bryant

"That must be quite a message in there," Polly interjected, "judging by the reaction on your face!"

Glenda shook her head and replied, "Oh? Uh...yeah...I guess. I just wasn't expecting it...I mean...I just don't know..."

"You don't know what? What is it?" Polly said as she took the card from Glenda's hand. Polly was a bit presumptuous, but Glenda didn't mind. Right now she needed a friend. "Wow! It's an invitation...a *personal* invitation from a *MAN*! Lucky you!" Then looking at the signature at the bottom she said, "Hey, isn't this the guy...the speaker they had last night?"

119

Glenda looked at Polly and smiled nodding in affirmation.

"So, are you going to meet him?" Polly continued.

Glenda looked concerned as she whispered to Polly, "I...I don't know. Do you think I should?"

"Are you *crazy*? Of course you should. From what I've heard, he sounds like a great guy. Besides, what do you have to lose?" Polly gathered their trays and helped Glenda to her feet, handing Glenda the willow cane, saying, "Let's go back to the pod so you can write out a response and get it to Sister Joan for delivery. Come on, girl! You have a reply to write!" She giggled, giving Glenda's arm a gentle squeeze.

Glenda sat on the edge of her bed with the small notebook in her hand; several balls of crumpled paper were tossed on the bed beside her. Who would think writing a simple reply could be so difficult! After several attempts she finally settled with the following:

Dear Mark,
Yes, I would like to talk with you, too.
See you at 11:00!
Glenda Ashbury

She read the response to Polly who smiled and said, "Perfect! It's simple and to the point...but friendly."

Glenda looked concerned and quickly asked, "Too friendly? Maybe I should re-write it!"

"No!" Polly exclaimed, "It's perfect. Let's just give it to Sister Joan." She folded the note and put it into the envelope sealing it tightly. Then handing it back to Glenda she stated, "Here's the start of something good...I just know it!"

******

Father Harris put the key into the lock of the front door to Glenda's house. He could hear the "thump" from the big cat as he jumped to the floor from the back of the sofa. The priest carefully unlocked the door, but the large cat unexpectedly darted out the front door, ran between Father Harris' legs, and into the street. As Father Harris turned and called for the cat to come back, a shiny black pick-up truck appeared in his peripheral vision.

It all happened in a matter of seconds; the squealing tires as the driver attempted to stop in time, and then the fatal thump from the impact. The big gray striped cat lay motionless on the pavement. Prince Snarls was dead.

A tall blonde woman quickly got out of the black shiny pick-up. She was obviously shaken as she approached the scene, saying, "I didn't see it until it was too late! I couldn't stop! Oh, God...is it dead? Did I kill it? Oh, Father...I am so sorry I killed your cat!"

Father Harris knelt down by the large gray striped mass of fur lying so still in front of him. As he gently lifted the limp, heavy cat from the pavement, his eyes filled with tears. He looked up at the tall blonde woman towering over him and said, "It was an accident. It isn't my cat. He was just in my care while his owner was away." Stroking the fur of the still warm body in his arms, he added, "Oh, Snarly...how do I tell Glenda?"

"Glenda?" The woman said suddenly, "Did you say Glenda? Would that be Glenda Ashbury?"

Father Harris looked up at the woman, tears filling his eyes, "Yes, that's right. Do you know Glenda? What is your name?"

The woman's eyes left the pitiful gaze of the priest's and she looked toward the ground. "Yes...yes, Father. I do know Glenda. My name is Bertha...Bertha

121

Carson. I work with Glenda at the plant." Bertha started to cry. "This is a terrible thing I've done. Glenda will be so angry with me..." she sobbed.

Father Harris cradled Prince Snarls in one arm and placing his hand on Bertha's shoulder, tried to console her, saying, "It was an accident, dear. You didn't do it intentionally. Why do you think Glenda would be angry with you?"

Bertha looked into the kind priest's eyes and said, "Because I'm a terrible person. I've treated Glenda badly...and now I've killed her cat! There is no way she'll believe it was an accident because of how I've treated her!" Bertha sobbed, "Oh, but Father...I really didn't mean for this to happen! How can I make her understand?" Tears trickled down her flushed cheeks as she hung her head in shame.

Father Harris could tell Bertha was truly remorseful about her behavior toward Glenda and the accident involving Prince Snarls. He lifted Bertha's chin so her eyes met his and said, "Bertha, we can not make anyone do anything. Not even God can do that, because of the free will he has given us. We are only responsible for our own behavior. We can not and should not try to control others. You have no control over the reaction Glenda will have when she finds out you accidentally killed her cat, but you do have control over your own behavior and reaction. No one can make you do, say, or be anything you don't already choose to do, say or be. Do you understand what I am saying to you?" Bertha nodded her head, "Yes, Father...I think so."

Father Harris continued, "If you are truly sorry...not just for this accident...but for the way you have treated Glenda, you need to let her know. God knows your heart and by His grace you will express it the right way to Glenda. Then you leave Glenda's response and reaction in God's hands." He smiled and added, "Remember, I was a witness to this accident. I can help with that explanation, but only you know how you have wronged Glenda in other ways. Are you prepared to ask Glenda's forgiveness?"

Bertha smiled as the tears welled up in her eyes, "Thank you, Father. I know what I need to do now."

Father Harris put his free arm around Bertha's shoulders and gave her a hug, saying, "I'll pray for you. If you ever need to talk to someone, come by St. Francis and visit me...anytime." Bertha returned to her truck and waved as she drove away.

Looking down at the big cat lying lifeless in his arm, Father Harris whispered, "Well, Snarly...I need to make the call to your mistress. I suppose I should find a nice box to place you in and a cold place to keep you until she comes home.

******

Sister Joan turned the corner of the long hallway leading from the first floor foyer. Pausing at the door of the private room where Mark Bryant temporarily resided, she knocked and whispered softly, "Mr. Bryant. It's Sister Joan. I have a message for you."

Mark quickly opened the door and smiled at the nun, saying, "Thank you, Sister...I hope it is good news."

"You're welcome, Mr. Bryant." Sister Joan responded and then winked, adding, "If I were a gambler, I'd be willing to bet it is!"

Mark closed the door and immediately opened the envelope. As he read the brief message written inside by Glenda he made a fist and drew it close to his side in a positive gesture, exclaiming, "YES!"

13.

The sound of the phone ringing could be heard faintly outside the heavy office door as Sister Joan inserted the key and turned the lock. Entering her small, cluttered, office, she lifted the receiver off the dated plastic phone base and breathlessly said, "Hello? Highland Monastery...Sister Joan speaking."

A familiar voice replied, "Sister Joan...this is Father Harris from Bakersfield..."

Sister Joan interrupted, "Yes, Father. What can I do for you?"

Father Harris took a deep sigh and continued, "Oh Sister, I have some sad news for one of your registered guests there...Glenda...Glenda Ashbury. Is there any way you could find her and allow me to speak with her? I'll gladly hold."

"Why yes, Father. She is actually staying right on this floor. I will go locate her and bring her to the office."

Father Harris gave another deep sigh, adding, "Bless you, Sister. That would be wonderful. I'll hold."

Sister Joan carefully placed the phone receiver down on a pile of papers strewn across her desk. Gazing up at the crucifix on the wall, she made the sign of the cross and said a quick prayer on Glenda's behalf as she went through the door and down the hall toward the guest area where she hoped Glenda would be. Entering the sleeping quarters, she could see that Glenda's bunk was neatly made up and the note she had brought her earlier was lying on the bed.

A voice called out from across the room, "Can I help you, Sister?" Polly was lying on her bunk reading.

Sister Joan turned, startled by the unexpected voice, "Oh my! Do you know where Glenda Ashbury is? I need to talk to her right away."

Sensing the urgency in the nun's voice, Polly placed the book down and quickly sat up, saying, "She just left to go down to the garden. I'm sure you can catch up with her..."

Sister Joan darted out the door and walked quickly down the hall toward the elevator. There stood Glenda. As the elevator doors opened Sister Joan called out, "Glenda! Glenda Ashbury!"

Glenda turned and noticed Sister Joan rapidly approaching her, nearly out of breath, and calling, "Come quickly, dear. There's an urgent phone call for you in my office."

Glenda stepped off the elevator and with a puzzled expression thought, "Who would be calling me?" But she followed the nun to the office. Glenda slowly lifted the receiver from its piled paper cushion and softly said, "Hello?"

"Oh, Glenda," the familiar voice came through the earpiece as Glenda sat down on the worn leather chair. She knew the news couldn't be good if Father Harris was trying to reach her during her retreat. Taking a deep breath, she continued, "Father Harris? What is it? Are you all right?" Glenda could tell by the tone of his voice there was something wrong.

There was a sigh as he softly said, "Glenda, I have some sad news..." Glenda's heart sank inside. She feared what the priest was about to say and wanted to drop the receiver back down on the phone base to disconnect the call; hoping it would delay the next moment of sadness, but she didn't. Taking a deep breath, she spoke softly, "What is it, Father? Has something happened to Prince Snarls?" She could hear the priest sniff as if wiping his nose.

"Glenda, when I went to the house this morning, Snarly darted out the door..."

Before Father Harris could finish, Glenda interrupted, "Oh, he does that sometimes. Don't worry;

125

he'll come back once he's done roaming." There was silence on the other end of the connection.

"Glenda, I'm afraid it is much worse than that," the Priest continued, "You see, he ran so fast...I called...but he wouldn't come back. Then he ran into the street. There was a truck coming...it couldn't stop. Oh Glenda, I am so sorry. It all happened so quickly."

Glenda sat listening as a tear slowly trickled down her cheek. She had to ask the next question, but she didn't want to, "Is he...is he dead? Is Snarly dead, Father?"

There was another deep sigh followed by another sniff as Father Harris replied, "Yes, Glenda. He died instantly. I'm so sorry."

Glenda turned the receiver away from her face and wept briefly. She took a deep breath and wiping the tears from her face said, "Where is he now?"

Father Harris quietly replied, "I placed him in a box in the cellar for now..."

He could hear Glenda's sobs as she responded, "I'm coming home. Thank you Father for caring for him; I'm so sorry this happened, but it was an accident. Sometimes accidents just happen. I need to take care of him, though, so I'm coming home."

Father Harris sighed and said, "I knew you would. I am so sorry, Glenda."

"I know," Glenda replied. "Good-bye, Father. I'll talk with you when I get home."

"Good-bye, Glenda," the priest replied, adding, "Please drive carefully down the mountain. Snarly is resting peacefully."

As Glenda hung up the phone, Sister Joan placed her hand on Glenda's shoulder saying, "I'll help you with your things."

******

The bright sunshine danced on the ripples of water created by the fountain in the middle of the garden out in front of Highland Monastery. Mark Bryant sat on the stone bench in the warmth of the late morning sun and glanced down at his watch. It was 11:45 and he started to wonder if somehow the message for Glenda to meet him at the fountain had gotten confused. As he looked toward the parking lot and the road leading out of the monastery grounds, he noticed the little yellow Volkswagen as it drove into the shroud of trees toward the main highway. A feeling of disappointment and concern replaced the anticipation and joy he was feeling.

"She had an emergency and had to go home," A voice called out from behind him. Startled, Mark turned and a small, thin woman with straight dark hair smiled at him. She reached her right hand forward, saying, "Hi, I'm Polly Petersen. Glenda and I shared a pod upstairs. She really wanted to come. Oh, she asked me to give you this." And she handed him a folded paper.

> **Dear Mark,**
> **I'm sorry I was unable to meet with you. There was an emergency and I had to leave early. Maybe someday our paths will cross again. Thank you for your words of encouragement and the kindness shown toward me. If you are ever in Bakersfield, Colorado, be sure to look me up and maybe we'll be able to have our talk.**
>
> **Glenda Ashbury**

127

Mark looked up from the note and asked Polly, "Is she all right? Do you know what happened?"

Polly sat on the bench by Mark and said, "She was so upset because her cat got out of her house and was hit by a truck and killed. That cat was like family to her and she wanted to go back to bury him." She tossed a pebble into the fountain and continued, "Glenda was looking forward to talking with you. I don't know her that well, but I can tell she is a good person. I hope you guys will meet again someday."

Mark folded the note and put it in his shirt pocket, saying, "Yeah, me too." Then turning to Polly he smiled and asked, "So, how far is Bakersfield from here?"

✲✲✲✲✲✲

Betty Ann Bryant loved the time she spent in the Briarwood Hills Nursing Home garden. She had made a request to the maintenance man to repair the trellis outside her room window. Now the winding rose had a good support and graciously displayed beautiful pink blossoms.

"You want to sit in the sun or shade?" The nurse aide asked as she wheeled Betty Ann down the sidewalk out side her room and into the garden courtyard.

The sun felt warm against Betty Ann's skin and soothing across her shoulders "I th-think I w-would l-like to s-sit in the s-sun f-f-for a wh-while," she replied.

"Well, okay, but not too long. Too much sun can cause wrinkles, you know!" the little aide said affectionately as she gave Betty Ann a hug.

Betty Ann patted the girl's arm gently and laughed, "Th-thanks f-for the w-w-warning, d-dear."

"I'll check on you in a little while, okay?" the aide said as she opened the garden door back into the nursing home.

Betty Ann adjusted the silk scarf that held the straw hat on her head, shading her face from the sun, and responded, "Th-that would b-be f-fine."

The little wrens were flitting back and forth; busily retrieving tender morsels for their demanding little ones. They returned to the tiny bird house which was mounted in the lush crab apple tree that softly shaded the bird bath. Betty Ann closed her eyes and leaned back into the soft cushion of the chair; breathing in deeply the sweet aroma of the flowers surrounding her. The warm sunshine felt soothing and comforting as she drifted off to sleep and dreams of years gone by.

$$******$$

The fragrant flowers of Exposition Park danced gracefully in the soft California breeze. The Christiansen girls often practiced there as small crowds gathered to watch them perform their acrobatic stunts and contortionist poses. The crowds would applaud and often remark on their incredible talent.

One day, a gentleman came forward from the crowd and approached Stella Jean, stating, "You girls are quite good and have an unusual talent." He reached into his suit jacket and pulled out a small card. Handing it to Stella and said, "My name is Mr. Gooseman and I represent *PIC Magazine*. Are you familiar with *PIC*?"

Stella Jean held the card and looked up at the tall attractive man and smiled, "Why yes, I am. I read it often."

Mr. Gooseman returned the smile, his thin black mustache twitching above his nearly absent upper lip. His dark eyes twinkled as he spoke, "That's great. We would like to offer you an opportunity of a life time. *PIC Magazine* is sponsoring a national amateur talent contest which is being held here in L.A. and at the World's Fair in New York City. We would like to invite you and your sister to participate in the competition."

Betty Ann looked at Stella, her eyes wide in wonder. Stella Jean's heart was pounding with excitement, but her voice was calm as she replied, "Yes, that does sound like a wonderful opportunity, but you will need to speak to our mother as she manages all the events in which we participate."

Mr. Gooseman was impressed by the young woman's professional demeanor. He gently tipped his felt hat and nodded, saying, "Have your mother call me, soon. We want to feature you along with other talented newcomers in our next issue." He gently shook the girls' hands and walked away.

Stella squealed with delight and threw her arms around Betty Ann. "Let's go tell Momma! We're going to be famous, Betty Ann...You'll see!" Stella put her hands on her younger sister's shoulders and repeated, "Betty Ann... Betty Ann..."

✳✳✳✳✳✳

Betty Ann was awakened by the gentle shaking from a hand on her shoulder and a familiar voice, repeating, "Betty Ann? Betty Ann?"

She opened her eyes and blinked briefly from the bright Nebraska sunlight. Looking up, she saw the smiling face of her sister, Stella Jean; leaning over her walker and gently shaking Betty Ann awake from her dream of the past.

"Are you okay, dear?" Stella asked softly.

"Oh, Y-yes, St-Stella. I w-was j-just having a w-w-wonderful dream," Betty Ann replied as she smiled up at her sister and gently patted the aged hand on her shoulder, "It w-w-was about th-that d-d-day when w-we were disc-c-covered in the p-p-park in L.A."

Stella laughed, "Oh my, dear. That was a very long time ago! I remember I thought we would become famous. I guess we did get our picture in *PIC Magazine*...not everyone can say that now, can they?"

"N-No they c-c-can't," Betty Ann answered, laughing. "And we b-b-both made *R-Ripley's B-Believe It or N-N-Not*, too. We've h-had s-s-some unique exp-p-periences, h-haven't w-w-we, St-Stella? Th-They even m-m-made us b-b-beauty queens."

Stella laughed and pushed her walker to the side as she sat on the bench next to Betty Ann's chair and exclaimed, "Look at us now!" Taking her sister's hand in hers, she added, "Cynthia and I have just a couple more days with you. What would you like to do?"

Betty Ann turned to her sister, replying, "I'm d-d-doing it," She slowly slipped her hand through her sister's arm and smiled.

* * * * * *

Father Harris decided to wait at Glenda's house for her return; knowing she might need a friend during this difficult time of loss. Glancing at the front bay window, he remembered the anxious antics of the big gray cat; pawing at the glass welcoming him. Now the window was empty. He slowly opened the door and sat down on the living room sofa. He noticed the scrapbook positioned on the trunk in front of him and thought, "I must remember to ask Glenda about this scrapbook and her relationship to Betty Ann Christiansen," Lifting the scrapbook to his lap, he carefully opened the pages.

Toward the back of the scrapbook, pressed between the pages, was an old magazine, dated June 25, 1940 and titled, *PIC Magazine.* It was folded in half and brittle with age, but Father Harris carefully opened it to the page marked with a yellow ribbon. Looking through the pictures, he recognized the two girls standing on their hands, back to back, and smiling. Below the picture was the following information:

Betty Ann and Stella Jean Christiansen (L.A.) are not mere acrobats; they are contortionists! Betty Ann has taken acrobatics from the time she could toddle. Stella,   broke Ripley's column, as the only person in the world who can stand on her hands and sit on her head at the same time! Although Stella and Betty have appeared at the Hippodrome, they are strictly "PIC" amateurs, who deserve your hearty applause.

132

He smiled and gently folded the old magazine and placed it back carefully between the pages of the Scrapbook. As he glanced out the window behind the sofa, the yellow Volkswagen pull up into the driveway and he silently prayed, "Lord, help Glenda through this painful time."

14.

Glenda sat on the back porch step staring at the small mound of fresh dirt rising above the green grass and scattered dandelions in her small back yard. The glass of ice tea sweated profusely in her hands as she slowly took a sip from the red and white striped straw. She raised the cool glass to her warm forehead and took a deep breath. Everyone she ever loved was now in the ground. She felt sad and very alone. Father Harris had offered to stay and help dig the hole for Prince Snarl's grave, but Glenda had wanted to bury him. She needed that time to complete her closure.

"I'll need to find a special marker for his little grave," she said, picking up her willow cane and carefully climbing the steps leading into her kitchen. Her heart sank as she glanced down at Snarly's food and water dishes on the floor at the end of the cabinet. She bent down and tenderly picked them up, carrying them over to the kitchen sink to dump the contents.

Slowly opening the end cabinet drawer, she removed the bag of kitty treats that Snarly loved so much. Glenda placed them, the dishes, a small toy jingle ball, and a little felt mouse in a plastic shopping bag. Removing the scrapbook and a candle from the top of the old trunk, she lifted the lid and placed the bag with its contents inside. Closing the lid, she set the candle and scrapbook back on top and sat down on the sofa. Leaning her head back against the patchwork quilt, she cried.

After a few minutes of cleansing tears, Glenda pulled a tissue from the box on the corner end table, wiped her tears, blew her nose and gave a big sigh. Glancing at the scrapbook on the trunk in front of her she smiled, saying, "Well, Betty Ann, let's see what you have been up to."

Glenda slowly turned the pages and it felt good to review the memories in the scrapbook once again. She had learned so much about this young girl, Betty Ann. The adventure with her mother and sisters had touched Glenda's life. Once again the thought of where Betty Ann might be today came to Glenda's mind.

"If Betty Ann is still alive, I'd love to reunite her with her scrapbook. I wonder how I can find out...or where to even begin?" She thought as she turned the page past the ocean drawings and the close-up photo of Betty Ann at the beach. She came upon the next page which included the letter from Margie. Glenda opened the letter and read how Margie's brother, Tim, had asked about Betty Ann. Drawn next to this part of the letter was a big red heart with the initials B.C. + T. B. printed inside it. There was a black arrow piercing the heart.

"Hmmmmm...Looks like Betty Ann had a pretty strong crush on this Tim guy," Glenda said as she picked up the envelope that was tucked away in the page binding. It was addressed to Miss Betty Ann Christiansen in Los Angeles, but the return address was Margie Bryant's in Briarwood, Nebraska. Once again Glenda wondered why Briarwood sounded so familiar, but her thoughts were abruptly interrupted when the phone rang in the kitchen. Placing the envelope back into the scrapbook, she rose and went into the kitchen to answer the phone.

"Hello?" She said, slightly out of breath.

"Glenda?" The familiar voice replied, "This is Father Harris. I just wanted to call and see how you are doing."

"Oh, I'm okay, Father. I got Snarly buried. Thank you for digging his grave for me," Glenda responded.

"Glenda, it was the least I could do. Are you sure you are all right?" Father Harris asked compassionately.

"Yes, Father...I mean it's hard and I miss him, but I'll be okay. I was just sitting and looking through this old scrapbook I have," Glenda said, hoping to change the subject.

"Oh, yes! The scrapbook! I've been going to ask you about that..." there was an excitement in Father Harris' voice as he continued, "How on earth do you know Betty Ann?"

Glenda, surprised by the question the priest just asked her, replied, "What do you mean? Why...do you...do you know Betty Ann?"

She heard the priest laugh and then he said, "Well, yes...I mean...sort of. It was a very long time ago. Do you have the scrapbook in front of you?"

Glenda was puzzled by Father Harris' response and slowly replied, "No...why?"

"Just go get it and I'll try to explain," he said.

Glenda placed the receiver down on the kitchen table and went into the living room to retrieve the scrapbook. Returning to the kitchen, she picked up the receiver and spoke, "Okay, Father, I have the scrapbook."

"Turn to the page that has the class picture," he instructed.

Glenda turned past the letter from Margie to the page which had the old class picture on it and she said, "Okay, Father, I found the class picture."

Father Harris laughed and said, "See the chubby little freckle-faced boy sitting on the ground in the front row?"

Glenda looked closely at the photo, "Yes, yes...I see him..."

"That's me!" Father Harris said still laughing.

"You're kidding...really?" Glenda was surprised. "You lived in California?"

Father Harris sighed, "Yes, a long time ago. Now, tell me...How do you know Betty Ann?"

Glenda laughed, "Oh, no, Father. I don't know her...I just bought this scrapbook at a thrift store and have enjoyed reading about Betty Ann and her mother and sisters. I can't believe you actually knew her! What a strange coincidence!"

Father Harris responded, laughing, "There are no coincidences in life...remember? You found that scrapbook for a reason."

Glenda hesitated, saying, "You really think so, Father? But what could the reason be? How do I know?"

Father Harris replied, gently, "Don't worry, Glenda. God has some kind of plan. When the time is right, you'll know."

Then Glenda quickly asked, "Tell me Father, do you know where Betty Ann might be now? I mean...do you think she is still alive?"

"Why, I don't know...she could be...I am!" and he laughed again. "Why do you want to know, Glenda?"

Glenda sighed, "Oh, I don't know...I guess I'd love to find her and reunite her with her scrapbook if she is still alive. Is that foolish, Father?"

"No, no...not at all, Glenda. I think it is a noble idea, but where would you start? What information do you have?

Glenda turned back through the pages, "Well, I know she lived in Briarwood, Nebraska. Her father was a shoemaker and she and her sister were acrobats and performed at fairs and carnivals. Her mother took the girls to California during the late thirties to find work performing. The scrapbook is a record of that adventure."

Glenda could hear Father Harris chuckle on the other end of the connection. He said, "I remember how she and her one sister would practice at the park and the bunch of us would all watch them. They could twist themselves into the strangest positions!"

Glenda noticed the envelope with the letter from Margie. Glancing at it, she remarked, "There's an envelope here with a return address from a Margie Bryant from Briarwood, Nebraska..."

Father Harris quickly interrupted, "Did you say Bryant...from Briarwood, Nebraska?"

Glenda was surprised by the excitement in the priest's voice and replied, "Yes, Father...Margie Bryant from Briarwood. Apparently she had a brother, Tim, who Betty Ann seemed to have a crush on..."

Her sentence was again interrupted by Father Harris' laughter. "Oh, my! That is something. Remember the speaker from the retreat you were just at? Mark...Mark Bryant? He is from Briarwood, Nebraska!"

Glenda gasped, "He is...Really?"

"Yes, yes...it says so right on your brochure from the retreat. Didn't you read it?"

Glenda remembered glancing at the brochure and now realized why the name of the town sounded so familiar to her.

"This is amazing, Father. Do you think that Mark could be related to Betty Ann?"

Father Harris couldn't help but notice the familiar way Glenda said Mark's name and remarked, "Glenda, did you have a chance to personally meet Mark Bryant this weekend?"

Glenda could feel her cheeks flush as she softly said, "Well...yes...yes, I did...but then I had to leave so abruptly. I thought I'd never get the chance to talk to him again."

"Well, maybe now you will," Father Harris replied gently and then repeated, "You'll know what you need to do when the time is right."

Glenda smiled, "Hmmmm....I guess you're right, Father, but for now I'm going to just focus on getting back to work and my same boring life. It's just a little lonelier now."

Father Harris sighed, "Well, Glenda, you always have me as a friend to talk to whenever you want. If there is ever anything I can do, just let me know, okay?"

"Okay, Father...thanks." After saying goodbye, Glenda hung up the phone and returned the scrapbook back to the trunk top. As she went to set it down, the copy of "PIC Magazine" slipped out from the back pages. She picked up the brittle magazine and turned to the marked page which revealed the picture of Stella Jean and Betty Ann. Glenda smiled, saying, "I'm going to find you, Betty Ann!"

It was very difficult for Mark to stay focused on his role as speaker and counselor for the remainder of the retreat. More than anything he wanted to leave and make the drive down the mountain to Bakersfield and try to find Glenda, but he had made a commitment and needed to stick to it. His services were desperately needed at the retreat as there were many attending who were recovering from problems in their lives. He kept the note from Glenda in his shirt pocket and in the evenings, while sitting down by the fountain he would think of her and pray for her and wonder if she was thinking of him.

******

Miss Swanson stepped into Betty Ann's room at the Briarwood Hills Nursing Home, "There's a phone call for you, Betty Ann. You can take it in my office if you'd like."

"Oh, th-thank you d-d-dear," Betty Ann replied as she maneuvered her wheel chair past the dresser and into the hall.

"Would you like me to help you?" Miss Swanson offered, observing the struggle Betty Ann was experiencing turning the large wheels at her side.

But Betty Ann knew she needed to try and do as much as she could herself and replied, "No th-thank you. I th-think I c-c-can m-m-manage. It j-j-just t-takes m-me a b-b-bit."

Miss Swanson smiled and said, "I'll let them know you're on your way." And she walked quickly down the hall to her office.

Betty Ann carefully picked up the receiver from the edge of the desk and breathlessly said, "H-H-Hello?"

"Mom? Mom, is that you? You sound winded. Were you doing cart wheels down the hallway again?" Mark said jokingly.

Betty Ann laughed, "Only in m-m-my d-dreams, d-d-dear. H-how about y-you?"

Mark laughed and said, "Yes, Mother, I have done a couple...and the crowd loved it! I always credit you for teaching me how, though!" He could hear his mother laugh and then he continued, "Are you enjoying your visit with Aunt Stella and Cynthia?"

"Oh, yes. It h-h-has b-been so g-g-good to s-see them again. W-w-we've b-been sharing old m-m-memories. Is th-there anything n-n-new with y-you?" Betty Ann knew her son so well and could detect a certain lift in his voice...an unexplained sound of joy.

Mark laughed, "You know me so well! As a matter of fact, Mom, I think I may have met someone special."

"I j-just knew it!" Betty Ann replied. "W-What is h-h-her n-name?"

"Her name is Glenda Ashbury, Mom. She has beautiful red wavy hair and the greenest eyes!"

"Sh-she s-s-sounds b-beautiful, M-Mark," Betty Ann said.

"She really is, Mom. And not just on the outside. She has a beauty within her, but we only just met. She had an emergency and had to leave the retreat early. I don't know when I'll get the chance to see her again."

Betty Ann could sense the disappointment and desperation in her son's voice and softly said, "Y-Y-You m-m-must f-find her, M-Mark. I can t-t-tell she has f-f-found a place in y-your heart."

Mark sighed, "I was hoping you'd say that, Mom. I'm going to take an extra day here in Colorado and drive down to Bakersfield where she lives. Is that okay with you?"

Betty Ann laughed, "Yes, d-dear. D-D-Don't w-w-worry about m-m-me. F-Folow your h-heart and f-find your little r-redhead!"

"Thanks, Mom. I'll call you again from Bakersfield," Mark replied.

"I'll l-l-look f-forward to it, S-Son. B-Be careful and g-g-good l-l-l-luck. I h-hope you f-find her and I'll p-pray that sh-she f-f-feels the s-same about y-you."

******

At the Highland Monastery, Polly Petersen looked down to the garden area from the window in the pod where she and Glenda shared their brief time together at the retreat. She could see Mark sitting on the stone bench, leaning forward with his elbows on his thighs. His hands were folded together and his head was bowed. Softly she whispered, "God, whatever he is asking for, please give it to him," A tear gently rolled down her cheek as she added,

"He is a good man and has helped so many...including me...please help him."

15.

The weekend was finally over and Glenda was attempting to move on with her life. Backing out of her driveway, she glanced up at the front window where her big gray cat always positioned himself to watch her drive away. Tears filled her eyes and she choked down the urge to sob. "It will get better," she whispered.

As Glenda entered the heavy gray doors leading into the plant, there was a strange hush among the group of women gathered around Bertha Carson.

"I wonder what big-mouthed Bertha is going to say to me. I'm just not sure I want to deal with her cruel remarks today," Glenda thought as Bertha's eyes met hers and she approached Glenda. But there was a difference in her eyes. They were softer and they looked so sad. Glenda stopped as the two women faced each other.

"Glenda," Bertha said softly, "there's something I must tell you, but first I just want to say how sorry I am for being so mean to you all these years."

Glenda was stunned and speechless, but she could tell Bertha was sincere and felt ashamed for calling her big-mouth in her thoughts.

"Please, let me finish," Bertha continued, "I have been a terrible person and I have done a terrible thing. I didn't mean to, but it is terrible just the same." Glenda looked puzzled. What could Bertha have done while Glenda was gone that was so bad?

Bertha looked down, shamefully and blurted out, "It was me...I did it...I was the one...but I didn't mean to...it was an accident..."

Glenda touched Bertha's arm to calm her and said, "What? What did you do?"

As Bertha looked up at Glenda there were tears in her eyes and she said softly, "I killed your cat. I'm so sorry."

143

Glenda was stunned and dropped her hand from Bertha's arm, "You? It was you?" And she turned her back to Bertha.

By now tears were slowly rolling down Bertha's flushed cheeks, "Yes, It was me...I'm so sorry. I didn't mean to. I don't blame you if you hate me and if you don't believe me...I mean...why should you? Especially after the way I've treated you always. But I had to tell you. And I had to let you know how sorry I am...not only for the accident...but for everything...I mean...EVERYTHING! And I just want you to know I won't be like that anymore...to you or anyone else!" She brushed the tears from her cheeks and Glenda turned to face her.

Although Glenda was still so hurt from the loss of Prince Snarls, she could see the remorse in Bertha's eyes. More importantly, she could sense the change in Bertha's heart.

She took a deep cleansing breath and said, "Bertha, it was an accident. No matter how mean you were to me before, I know you didn't purposely kill my cat. It hurt me deeply to lose Prince Snarls, but it makes me so happy to see you have had a change of heart and realized how hurtful you were." She tenderly touched Bertha's arm and said, "I forgive you...for everything."

Instead of going to her regular place on the line, Glenda went to the personnel office. During her evening prayers the night before an idea came to her. She had decided to request some immediate time off and felt she deserved it after so many years. Her conversation with Father Harris, along with the recent information she had gained about Betty Ann and the scrapbook, had convinced her that she needed to make a trip to Nebraska, to the little town of Briarwood. She wanted to try and find out whatever happened to Betty Ann Christiansen and her family. Maybe, just maybe, she would be able to reunite her with the scrapbook. Maybe, just maybe, she would

144

finally be able to have that talk with Mark Bryant...if she could locate him, too.

Glenda smiled as she walked from the personnel office with her approved leave forms in her hand. She got into her little yellow Volkswagen and placed the willow cane on the passenger seat. Turning the key to the ignition, the familiar lyrics of " Hey Jude" played loud and clear and she smiled, singing along.

******

Mark tried not to speed as he maneuvered the rental car around the curves of the mountainous road from Highland. He was on his way to Bakersfield; determined to locate the woman who stole his heart in just a few brief moments. Polly had provided him with Glenda's address and he decided to surprise her. The thought occurred to him that he should probably call first, but he wanted to see the surprised expression on Glenda's face when he showed up at her door.

He recreated the scene over and over in his mind; imagining each moment. Always the version was a happy one with Glenda's face flushing the way it first did when their eyes met in the parking lot of the monastery. "Those beautiful green eyes," he thought, as he noticed the sign welcoming travelers to Bakersfield.

After driving around the small community for several minutes; Mark finally surrendered to his frustration and stopped to ask directions to the street where Glenda lived. As he pulled into the corner Gas Stop, he approached a shiny black pick-up, with a tall blonde woman effortlessly loading cases of pop into the back end.

Lowering the window Mark asked, "Excuse me, can you tell me where this street is?" He handed the woman the slip of paper with Glenda's address.

Bertha smiled at the good looking man in the car and replied, "Sure, I know where this is. Follow me. I'll take you there." She handed the paper back to Mark.

The black pick-up drove away slowly as Mark got out of his car and waved at the nice woman who took time to lead him to what he hoped was his dream. The little house before him looked strangely quiet and there was a rolled newspaper still lying on the porch. Mark rang the door bell. No response. He knocked on the door, thinking maybe the door bell was broken, but still no response. "I should have called," he said sadly as he walked back to his car. "Maybe she just went out for a while and will be back again soon. I'll go get a bite to eat and try again later."

Driving down Main Street, Mark noticed the little café and decided to go in for a late lunch. The row of bells hanging on the door jingled as Mark entered the café. All faces turned to see who the stranger was coming into the room.

A familiar voice called out, "Hey! Mark...Mark Bryant! What are you doing here?"

Mark turned and saw a priest waving at him from a stool at the counter. Mark politely waved back, but must have had a puzzled expression on his face because the priest said, "You probably don't remember me. We worked at a retreat together some time ago...in western Nebraska. I don't think we ever officially met, however." He reached his hand out to shake Mark's hand, saying "I'm Father Harris."

Mark remembered that retreat and the familiar smile and jovial laugh of the old priest and replied, "Father Harris, yes...it's good to see you again. That was a few years back, wasn't it?"

146

The priest laughed and patted his large belly saying, "A few years and a few less chocolate shakes, too! So, what brings you to Bakersfield?"

Mark sat on the stool next to the priest and ordered a cheeseburger and diet soda. Turning to Father Harris, he said, "Actually, Father, I'm looking for someone. Perhaps you know her...Glenda Ashbury?"

Father Harris laughed and patted Mark on the back saying, "Good for you, young man! I'm sure she would like to see you, only..." he paused.

"Only...what?" Mark replied, "Tell me, Father...what is it?"

"Well, she left this morning to go out of town. As a matter of fact she should be flying out about now," the priest said as he glanced at his watch and took another sip from his chocolate shake.

"Left? Left for where?" Mark asked anxiously. He was a little annoyed by the smile the priest was displaying.

Father Harris put his arm around Mark's shoulders, whispering, "To find you. She is headed to Briarwood."

******

At the airport, Glenda sat and waited for her plane to board. Sitting across from her was an attractive older woman with a walker. A young woman was seated next to her. They were looking through pictures and talking about the wonderful visit they had with their sister and aunt.

Glenda smiled at them, asking, "Where are you headed?"

The older woman smiled back, replying, "We're going back to California, but had a lay over with our flight from Nebraska where I was visiting my ill sister. How about you, dear? Where are you headed?"

Glenda smiled and looked out the large window at the plane sitting ready to board. She stroked the scrapbook which was hidden inside a plastic bag on her lap and said, "I'm going to a reunion in Nebraska."

The older woman smiled and commented, "A reunion. Oh, that is wonderful. Will everyone be there?"

Glancing back at the two women, Glenda responded, "I hope so."

★★★★★★

Betty Ann was informed she had a telephone call waiting for her at the nurses' station, so she slowly made her way down the hall. Making the chair move was becoming easier for her.

"It's your son, Betty Ann," the nurse aide said, handing the receiver to Betty Ann as she approached the station.

"Hello, Mark," Betty Ann said without hesitation.

"Hi, Mom," Mark responded; there was a tone of disappointment and anxiousness in his voice.

"W-What h-h-happened, dear?" Betty Ann asked. She heard a big sigh at the other end of the line.

"Well," Mark continued, "I got to Bakersfield and finally found her house, but she wasn't there. So I went to eat, thinking she'd come home later, but I found out, from the priest here...Father Harris...that she has left town!"

"L-Left town? Wh-Wh-Where did sh-she g-go?" Betty Ann asked.

"That's the amazing thing, Mom! She is on her way to Briarwood to find me!" Mark responded excitedly.

148

"She took a flight out of Denver. I assume she will fly into Omaha and probably rent a car. I'm going to head home from here, but I might not be able to get there until late tonight, so I won't come see you until tomorrow. Is that all right?"

Betty Ann laughed at her son's enthusiasm and said, "Th-that's f-fine, Mark. D-Drive s-safely...and d-d-don't w-worry. It w-will all c-come together, y-you'll s-see."

"I hope you're right, Mom," Mark responded, "I need to get on the road now. See you tomorrow!"

Betty Ann smiled at the nurse aide and handed her the receiver, saying, "Mark w-will be h-home tom-morrow. It w-will b-b-be g-good t-to have h-him b-back."

The nurse aide took the receiver and patted Betty Ann's hand saying, "I'm happy for you , hon. Your son is a good man. He'll make some woman a fine husband someday."

Betty Ann smiled and responded, "I h-hope so."

16.

Glenda glanced out the window as the large plane taxied down the tarmac and to its holding position; preparing for take off. The scrapbook was nestled securely at her feet and under the seat in front of her as she anticipated the take off. This was her very first flying experience and she was a little nervous.

The couple sitting next to her were holding hands and strangely quiet. The man sat on the aisle seat and the woman sat next to Glenda in the middle. She and Glenda had confused their seat belts earlier and when Glenda looked up, she noticed the redness and puffiness in the woman's eyes as she presented a weary smile.

Leaning forward, the man asked Glenda, "Is this your first time flying?"

Glenda smiled and released the tightly twisted tissue clutched in her hands, "Does it show?"

"Maybe a little," the man answered, adding, "Are you staying in Nebraska or flying on to somewhere else?"

"I'm going to stay in Nebraska for a while," Glenda responded. Suddenly, she could hear the great engines roar as the plane began its take-off. Glenda gripped the arm rest and sat straight in her seat; once more checking the seat belt fastened securely around her waist as the flight attendant had instructed. "I guess we're taking off," she said, smiling nervously at the couple.

Once the plane reached its cruising altitude and the fasten seat belt light was turned off, Glenda leaned forward and pulled the scrapbook out from under the seat in front of her. She gently removed it from the plastic bag and set it on her lap. She carefully turned the pages and reflected on all she had learned of Betty Ann and her family. Toward the back of the scrapbook, there was an old high-way map tucked between two pages. Glenda slowly unfolded the brittle map and noticed that Route 66 from California to

Oklahoma was highlighted with red crayon, which left a dim trace of pink on any areas of the map it came in contact with. The woman next to Glenda smiled as Glenda attempted to refold the map back to its original form.

Realizing Glenda was struggling to get the old map to cooperate, she softly said, "Here, let me help you. I've always been pretty good at getting these things back together."

Glenda hesitated, but gently handed the map to the woman; reasoning it might be a good distraction from what ever was making her so sad. She watched as the woman skillfully and carefully refolded the old map to its original form and then handed it back to Glenda with the same weary smile she displayed earlier. This time her hazel eyes were clearer and less red. Glancing down at the scrapbook opened across Glenda's lap, she said, "That looks really old. Is it a family heirloom?"

Glenda smiled as she placed her hand tenderly on the pages in front of her, "I suppose it would be a family heirloom. I guess that's why I hope I will be able to find the owner or family it belongs to."

The woman looked surprised, "You mean it isn't yours? I mean...your families' heirloom?"

Glenda could feel her cheeks flush and she didn't know why, but suddenly she felt a little shameful. She slowly closed the pages and said, "No...it isn't about my family...actually I bought it at a thrift store. I've been going through it and...well...enjoying the stories."

"Really?" The woman replied, "That's fascinating! What an amazing find! I love thrift stores, too!"

Relieved, Glenda reopened the scrapbook and briefly described what she had learned about Betty Ann and her family to the woman and her husband. Reaching the final pages, she found a note from Betty Ann which read:

We're going home! I am so happy! These past eight months in California have been fun, but I am so anxious to get home and see my Dad and Margie again! I think her brother Tim will be surprised to see how much I've changed! I will miss the new friends I made here...especially Tommy Harris, because he was always so funny and nice to everyone. And I'll miss the beautiful ocean. Someday, I hope I can come back.

Scattered across those final pages were various photographs of the Christiansen women. There was a beautiful picture of Stella Jean and a much more mature looking Betty Ann. Both were wearing formal gowns and had sashes draped from their shoulders, across their front and extending to just past their opposite hip. Written across the front of Stella Jean's sash were the words, *Miss Los Angeles* and across Betty Ann's were the words, *Little Miss California*. Glenda smiled at the thought of them finding their fame.

There were many pictures from the drive back to Nebraska along Route 66. Glenda admired the one of Betty Ann standing in front of the Oklahoma State Capitol Building and pointing to a large oil well on the front lawn. Betty Ann had matured during her time in California and had changed from a little girl to a young woman.

"Wow, they really are beautiful!" The woman next to Glenda said as she glanced at the photos.

"Yeah," Glenda said, "and they were very talented, too."

"I can see that in these photos," the woman responded as they glanced at the various pictures and articles about Stella and Betty Ann, attached to the pages. "I sure hope you can find them. Do you have any idea where to start your search?"

Glenda smiled as she turned the page which revealed her best clue yet. In the center of the page was a square paper surrounded by hand painted stars. Printed on the paper was the following information:

This scrapbook belongs to:
BETTY ANN CHRISTIANSEN
527 MAPLE STREET
BRIARWOOD, NEBRASKA
"A Wandering Rose"

"Briarwood?" The woman exclaimed, "That's where we are headed! What a coincidence!"

Glenda closed the scrapbook and turned to the woman, saying, "Don't you know there are no coincidences in life?" She smiled, asking, "What is in Briarwood for you?"

The woman sighed as the man next to her gently took her hand. Her eyes filled with tears as she said, "We are going to a funeral."

"I'm so sorry!" Glenda stated and continued, "Friend or family?"

The woman and man both smiled as she replied, "I guess you could say its family...although we never really met. I'm going to my biological mother's funeral. She gave me up at birth. I just found out about her and that she was very sick. She was living at the Briarwood Nursing Home. We were hoping to at least meet her before she died, but now we are going to her funeral instead." The man gently raised the woman's hand to his lips and kissed the back of it as she continued, "The director contacted me and stated she had some things that Laura...my mother...wanted me to have." A tear slowly rolled down the woman's beautiful brown cheek.

Their conversation was interrupted by an announcement from the pilot stating the plane was approaching Epply Airfield in Omaha, Nebraska. Glenda put the scrapbook back into the plastic bag and placed it

153

under the seat in front of her and prepared for landing in Nebraska.

******

"Betty Ann," Miss Swanson called, gently knocking the door frame leading into the small room at the Briarwood Hills Nursing Home.

"C-Come in d-dear," Betty Ann responded, turning her wheel chair toward the door and away from the easel and painting in front of her.

Miss Swanson stepped into the room carrying a large canvas. When she turned the canvas around, Betty Ann recognized it as the one she had given to Laura.

"Betty Ann, I'm sorry to have to tell you this, but Laura passed away suddenly."

Betty Ann set her brush on the paint blotched palette, balancing on the night stand. Looking at the canvas which Miss Swanson laid on the bed, she took a deep breath and then sighed, "She l-loved that p-p-painting,"

"She really did, Betty Ann. It was good of you to give it to her," Miss Swanson said.

Betty Ann looked puzzled and asked Miss Swanson, "W-Why is it h-h-here?"

Miss Swanson was surprised, replying, "Well...I guess we just assumed you would want it back...don't you?"

Betty Ann rolled her chair over to the bed and lifted the canvas handing it back to Miss Swanson, "No...N-n-no, I d-d-don't! It's n--no longer m-m-mine. Isn't th-there s-s-someone she kn-knew that y-y-you can g-g-g-give it to?"

Miss Swanson hesitated as she lifted the canvas from Betty Ann's aged hands. She held the canvas in front of her and smiled, saying, "Well...yes...there might be

154

someone...and she should be here soon. Perhaps she would like this memento from her mother." Miss Swanson noticed the surprised look on Betty Ann's face, adding, "Oh...you didn't know!"

"Sh-she h-h-had a d-d-daughter?" Betty Ann asked, wheeling her chair around the bed and closer to Miss Swanson, who looked like she had just revealed something that, perhaps, she wasn't supposed to.

Sitting on the edge of the bed, Miss Swanson gently took Betty Ann's hand in hers, saying, "Yes, dear...I'm sorry. I thought maybe she had shared this with you.

We didn't even know about the daughter either until recently. Laura left a note addressed to her caregivers at Briarwood requesting her things go to her daughter when she died. Laura and her daughter never really met because the baby girl was surrendered at birth and adopted. I know this because Laura's daughter contacted me after months of searching for her birth mother. It was so difficult to have to call her so soon and tell her that Laura...her mother...had died suddenly.

Tears welled up in Miss Swanson's eyes as she continued, "The daughter and her husband are flying here to get the few things Laura left behind...and to attend her funeral in the morning. It will be a sad reunion"

Betty Ann reached over to the night stand and pulled a tissue from the pretty flowered box, handing it to Miss Swanson, saying, "You p-p-ut that p-p-painting with the r-r-rest of Laura's th-things and m-m-make sure her d-d-d-daughter gets it, p-p-please. I w-w-would like for h-h-her to h-have it. Maybe it will help bring some joy to a sad reunion."

Miss Swanson dabbed the tears from her eyes with the tissue, and stated, "That is sweet of you, Betty Ann. I'm sure she will love it."

17.

"Hi, Mom," Marks voice greeted his mother as he drove his rental car down interstate 80 east across Nebraska toward home. There was interference in the cell phone connection but he wanted to let his mother know where he was while on the road.

"Mark? Is th-that you?" Betty Ann asked as she clasped the receiver tightly in her hands, "I c-can b-b-barely h-hear you, d-dear."

Mark switched the cell phone to his other ear as if the distance between one side of his head to the other would make the cell phone signal stronger, "Sorry, Mom. I'm on the road. I just wanted to call and let you know where I am...okay?"

"Ok-kay, d-d-dear. It w-w-will b-b-be g-good to have y-you h-home again," Betty Ann shouted, hoping Mark could hear her, "P-please drive c-carefully, M-mark."

The cell phone signal was getting weak as Mark responded, "I will, Mom. See you in the morning..." And then the call was dropped.

Betty Ann smiled as she handed the receiver back to the nurse aid, saying, "M-my s-s-son will be h-home tonight...b--but I w-w-won't s-see him until t-t-tomorrow."

"I'm glad he'll be home soon, Betty Ann. I bet you've missed him while he was gone," she said, helping Betty Ann turn her wheel chair around and through the office doorway, "You want some help back to your room?"

Betty Ann just smiled and waved her hand saying, "No, no, d-dear, I'm f-fine, thank you j-just the s-same." Slowly pushing the big side wheels on the chair forward with her small hands, and carefully shuffling her feet along the floor, she used each step to help pull the chair along. Her feet and hands were beginning to work together more effectively and slowly she could feel her strength returning.

The physical therapist even had her standing briefly that morning. Maybe she would be able to go home to her little house on Maple Street soon. Making her way back to her room in her temporary home, she recalled the same feeling of excitement and anticipation from a memory of a very special home coming many years ago.

******

The days were warm in California. There wasn't much variation in climate from one season to the next; not like the seasons in Nebraska. In this part of California it was always like spring or summer with the occasional rain.

Betty Ann missed the beautiful fall colors of autumn and the piles of snow in winter. It was spring now and she imagined how the landscape around Maple Street was probably changing. The spring flowers would be pushing up soon through the dried brown leaves in the flower beds her mother had planted. Soon the winding rose bush would find its way up the trellis mounted against the house. She imagined her father cleaning the leaves and debris out of the little pond in the back yard and filling it with fresh water again.

Lying in the warm sand and listening to the waves collide with the shore, she thought about what an incredible experience the past eight months had been. It was amazing to have lived in such a completely different part of the country and it would be difficult to say good bye to all her new friends when the time came for her to return to Nebraska. She wondered when that time would come. Her thoughts were rudely interrupted when she was suddenly shocked by the impact of cold water against her sun-warmed skin.

"Tommy Harris...you rat!" Betty Ann shrieked as she sat up and saw the red-headed boy running away laughing; empty bucket in hand. Jumping to her feet, she quickly caught up to him and playfully pushed him over into a splashing wave. The rest of the gang laughed as she and Tommy splashed each other in the cool water of the Pacific Ocean.

It was the end of the school year and Betty Ann and her friends were gathering at the beach. Not only were they celebrating another year of school over, but also the beginning of a new stage of life...junior high. How they had changed this past year. They weren't little kids any more...but not yet grown up either. It was that in-between stage.

Returning to the apartment later that day, Betty Ann climbed the steps to the small upper-level flat and hung her damp towel on the rail outside. "I'm home!" she announced coming through the door. Stella Jean and Ida Mae were sitting on the bed. Her mother was sitting on a wooden folding chair across from her sisters, reading a letter and paused when Betty Ann came through the door.

"Hi, dear," Mary said looking up from the letter and smiling, "How was the beach?"

"It was fun," Betty Ann responded, glancing at her sisters, "What's going on?"

"Sit down, Betty Ann," Mary said as she patted the area on the bed next to Ida Mae, "I was reading a letter from your father."

Betty Ann sat down slowly on the bed and cautiously asked, "Is he...is everything, okay?"

Mary smiled and continued to read, "The house is painted now and the flowers are starting to come up. Business has been much better as I have been supplying the state workers with their work shoes and boots. I hope you are ready to come home. I miss you all so much. I am going to wire you some money to help you with your trip home. Please come soon. I love you all...Dad."

Mary lowered the letter to her lap and looked into the eyes of her three beautiful daughters, saying, "Pack your things, girls! We're going home!" The girls sprung from the bed and hugged each other with joy. What a wonderful statement that was!

Saying good-bye is never easy. They had all made such good friends in California. Mrs. Barns from the bakery below their apartment sent them on their way with bags and baskets of fresh rolls and bread. Betty Ann's friends gave her a new address book with all their addresses filled in. Ida Mae's best customers at the drive-in all pitched in and gave her a jar full of extra tips and Stella Jean made a promise to a certain young man to return after she completed high school. Uncle Jim and Aunt June came to see them off on their journey back to Nebraska. He made certain the old Plymouth coup was in good shape for the journey, paid for their first tank of gas and encouraged Mary to take Route 66 - East as far as she could, explaining, "It was the most important highway at that time."

Betty Ann didn't notice much along the drive home because she was just so excited about getting back to Nebraska. One thing she did think was different and unusual was when they got to Oklahoma and she saw an oil well in the yard of the state capital building.

"Oh, Momma...can we please stop and take a picture of it?" Betty Ann said excitedly.

Along the rest of the drive, there were many nice, new, family camping areas and motels. The towns they passed through were doing all they could to attract the travelers who drove along Route 66.

When they finally pulled up in front of the little house on Maple Street, Betty Ann thought her heart was going to leap right out of her chest from the excitement.

She could hardly wait for the door of the old Plymouth coup to open so she could run into the arms of her father. Burying her face into his chest, she breathed in deeply the familiar scent of him and cried, "Daddy...we're home! We're finally home!"

John Christiansen hugged his daughter and reached out his arm to Mary who was quickly approaching. He bent down and kissed her warmly and said, "Welcome home!" Looking down at Betty Ann he added, "I think there's someone else who is anxious to meet you," and he pointed toward the house.

Betty Ann turned her attention toward the freshly painted house and saw a white ball of fur with black eyes and a pink tongue running toward her on short little legs with a curled tail wagging rapidly across its back.

"A dog! You got us a dog!" Betty Ann squealed with delight, "Oh, Daddy, he's so cute!"

John hugged his other two daughters and said, "Yes he's cute, but he needs some training and a name. I'll leave that up to you, Betty Ann."

The puppy wiggled and jumped straight up in the air as if it were on a spring. "I'm going to call him Jack...Jumping Jack!" Betty Ann said as she took the wiggly puppy in her arms; letting him lick her face repeatedly.

"Betty Ann! Betty Ann!" a familiar voice called from the distance, "You're finally home!" Betty Ann could see Margie running up the street to greet her. Cruising by slowly in his father's Ford pick-up was Margie's brother, Timmy Bryant. He looked so much older behind the wheel and driving. The look on his face made Betty Ann realize that she must look a little older, too, even if she was holding a furry, wiggly puppy.

It was a wonderful reunion. Betty Ann knew she would cherish the memory of it always in her heart. Living

160

in California was a wonderful adventure, but she was so glad to be home again.

$$*\,*\,*\,*\,*\,*$$

Glenda gathered the scrapbook, along with the carry on bag from the overhead compartment. Supporting the additional weight with the help of the diamond willow cane, she proceeded down the aisle of the plane to the exit door leading to Epply Airport.

"Welcome to Nebraska," the smiling flight attendant said as she assisted Glenda through the doorway. Glenda could feel the humidity of the hot mid-summer air as she exited the plane and into the long tunneled hallway leading to the airport.

"Good luck with your search!" A voice called out from behind her.

Glenda turned and looked back. She saw the couple who sat with her on the flight waving as they wrestled their bags from the overhead compartment. Glenda smiled and waved back.

Acquiring her rental car and maneuvering her way out of the airport was easier than Glenda anticipated. The sun was setting as she headed out of the city and past miles of corn fields on her way to Briarwood. The scrapbook lay on the passenger seat beside her, securely wrapped inside the plastic bag. Anticipating the new adventure she was undertaking, Glenda wondered if she would finally find what she was searching for in Nebraska.

18.

The Bee-Line Motel in Briarwood was a quaint family operated business. It sat on the edge of town and had a flashing neon sign displaying an impish bee whose wings appeared to flutter with the movement of the lights. As Glenda turned into the gravel circular drive and parked under the canopy over-hang in front of the office, she smiled at the elderly woman at the desk waving at her from inside. The welcome sign in the window read, *VACANCY*.

"Good evening, Miss," the woman greeted Glenda cheerfully as she approached the check-in counter, "You need a room?"

"Yes, yes, I do," Glenda replied, adding, "Do you have weekly rates?"

The woman stood up from her stool and smiled, saying, "Why, yes...yes we do. It is seventy five dollars a week, plus tax...and that includes full maid service. Now if you want a kitchenette it will be a bit more...ninety dollars a week...but we also have free cable!" She looked down at the cane that Glenda was leaning on and added, "I do have one available...and it is on the ground floor...so you don't have to climb any steps..."

Glenda appreciated the consideration the woman was trying to show, but felt a little uncomfortable with the added attention and quickly responded, "That would probably be best...the kitchenette, I mean. I'll take it." Reaching into her front jean pocket, she pulled out some slightly crumpled bills; a fifty and two twenties.

Glenda wasn't one for carrying a purse, but she did have a little red wallet that fit nicely into her back hip pocket of her jeans. It was all she needed to carry as her tube of lip gloss fit easily in her other front pocket and that was the extent of her make-up accessories. She had a natural beauty that others noticed but she didn't recognize.

"I just need you to fill out this information form for me, dear. Are you here on business or pleasure?" The woman asked as she handed Glenda a pen with a large pink silk flower attached to the end of it. Glenda laughed as she took the pen and the woman explained, "I make the pens that way so folks don't take them away. It's amazing how many pens I was losing each week until I did that."

"Good idea." Glenda replied as she filled out the form with her name, address, and driver's license number. She stepped away from the desk to glance at the rental car on the driveway to see what the license plate number was. After signing her name and date, she handed the completed card and the decorated pen back to the woman, saying, "I guess you could say I'm here for pleasure." She was going to offer more information, but changed her mind.

The woman returned the pen to the small glass clown-shaped dish on the counter which held other flower decorated pens and said, "Well, welcome to Briarwood. If I can be of any assistance, just let me know. I've lived here just about all my life...so I know most everyone. I don't meddle in other folks' business though...but I do know the best places to see and where to get a good meal out if you're interested. All you got to do is ask," She smiled, handed Glenda her room key and continued, "Your room is just three doors down. You'll probably want to bump the air a little so it kicks on to cool the room down. I don't keep them running when the room is empty. There's clean towels in the bathroom, but if you need more, just ask. Have a good stay."

Glenda took the key and turning to leave she noticed a newspaper stand with the *Briarwood Enterprise*, the local paper, displayed. She handed the clerk fifty cents and took a paper and smiled, saying, "Thanks again. By the way...Is there a grocery store close by where I can buy a few things?"

"Sure, we have a couple of them but the local market is just up the street and past the first stop light. You'll see it on the right side of the road...Stewart's Market. They have the best meat in town and really fresh produce...mostly locally grown. Be sure to tell them you're staying at the Bee-Line. Maybe they'll give you a good deal," she said laughing.

"Thanks...I will. You have been very helpful," Glenda said, tucking the paper under her arm and heading out the door. It was getting late and she was feeling a little hungry so she retreated to her room to unpack her bag and turn on the air conditioner. The room would have time to cool down while she shopped for a few groceries at Stewart's Market.

* * * * * *

Driving down the interstate alone gave Mark plenty of time to think about Glenda and what he would say to her when they met. It would be several hours before he would get to Briarwood and too late to try to find her. He reasoned that she probably wouldn't leave town though until she had found him, since that is what Father Harris said she was doing. Focusing on the road ahead, he wished he had flown to Colorado rather than rented a car to drive but he had thought the drive would be relaxing. He didn't care much for flying...but now he just couldn't get back fast enough.

"I wonder where Glenda is staying in Briarwood," he thought. "I'm glad Briarwood isn't a large city like Omaha or Lincoln. At least we should be able to meet up with each other somehow. I still can't imagine her making the trip to Briarwood just to see me. Maybe God has finally heard my prayers and is sending me someone that I can share my life with." He shook his head as if to wake himself from a trance, stating, "Wait a minute...what am I saying? Am I being serious here? We barely know each other and already I am making plans for us to be together. Lord, I need your help here...help me to keep it real and not get too carried away." Then he pictured her green eyes and wavy red hair and his heart skipped a beat.

******

The room was much cooler when Glenda returned from the market with her bag full of groceries to sustain her during her stay in Briarwood. She was going to take a drive around town to see if she could find Maple Street, but decided it was getting dark and that morning would be a better time to do some searching. Once the groceries were put away she kicked off her shoes and stretched out on the bed. Reaching to turn on the overhead lamp, she noticed the *Briarwood Enterprise* newspaper which she had purchased laying on the night stand.

"Let's see what's happening in this little town," she said, unfolding the paper to reveal the front page. In the lower left hand corner was a listing of the names featured on the obituary page of the paper. Glenda glanced at the names and noticed one that read Laura Gibson. She quickly turned to obituary page and read the short article. The memorial service was listed for tomorrow.

"That's her...that's the mother of the woman at the airport. Oh, why didn't I get her name! I'm just sure of it. I know her mother's name was Laura and that she was a resident at the Briarwood Home. It must be her. It says here the memorial service is tomorrow morning, at Petersen

165

Mortuary, and that she will be buried at the Briarwood Cemetery. I wonder if I should go and show my respects. I don't even know her...but I feel so bad for her daughter...and I'm sure hardly anyone will be there to show their support. It's not like I have pressing plans...I mean, yes I'm anxious to find Mark and talk with him....he'll probably think I'm nuts, anyway...and I want to try and find Betty Ann...but something tells me I should go to this. So, I think I will." She glanced through the paper at the other articles and ads, but was too tired to take much interest in anything. Slipping off her clothes and putting on her oversized t-shirt, she climbed into bed. It had been a long day and she was ready for some sleep.

Before drifting off she prayed, "Lord, thank you for a safe flight. Be with Laura and her family. Help me find Betty Ann...and...Mark...and...."

Mark entered Briarwood from the west side of town. Passing the Bee-Line Motel, the thought occurred to him that Glenda was probably sound asleep somewhere in Briarwood and he didn't have a clue where. He was anxious to get home, but wondered if he would be able to get any sleep due to the anticipation he felt of finally getting to talk to her again. He hadn't felt this way for a very long time.

Driving past Steward's Market the large sign out front had just shut off. "Must be eleven o'clock," he said, "I guess I should drive by Mom's house just to check and make sure everything is okay. She'll ask me in the morning if I did."

Turning left at the next street up and driving two blocks to Maple Street, he turned left again. About half-way up the street was the little tan house with the lamp glowing in the front window. Mark had set it on a timer so it would go off at eleven-fifteen and as he parked his car at the curb the light went out.

He walked up to the house and unlocked the front door. The house was quiet as he turned on the lights and walked through. His mother's things were all just as she had left them and waiting for her return.

"I hope she can get back here soon," Mark said, looking around the room, "It would be hard for her to not be able to come home again."

As he left and locked the door, he looked back on the little house in the moonlight and prayed, "God, please let Mom come home again."

He drove to his apartment and parked the rental car next to his mother's blue car. "Finally home," he said, with a sigh, walking up to the entrance of his apartment building, "Home sweet...apartment."

Betty Ann turned and glanced at the alarm clock on her night stand. It was midnight. "Mark should be home by now and he will call me in the morning," she thought. The summer moon was casting a soft glow around her room. "This place isn't so bad," she thought, "I guess I could probably make this my home...but, God, I hope you'll let me go home to my little house on Maple Street again...for just a little while longer."

She gently folded her hands and continued in thoughtful prayer, "Dear God, please welcome Laura to

167

your home in heaven. Thank you for the opportunity to know her. Give her daughter peace during this difficult time. And God, please help Mark find his little red-head. Amen."

Betty Ann closed her eyes and slept peacefully.

19.

Glenda was awakened by the sound of a car door slamming outside her motel room window. Walking slowly to the window and peeking through the mini-blinds, she observed one of the other guests was loading things in their car and getting ready to leave. The bright sunshine caused her eyes to squint and there was a haze in the air as she checked out the surrounding landscape.

"Looks like another hot and humid day in Nebraska," she said, releasing the blinds and stretching. She couldn't believe how well she slept. "I don't think I even sleep that well at home," she remarked, making her way into the small bathroom and turning on the shower.

The steam quickly filled the room and Glenda pulled off the big t-shirt and carefully stepped into the shower; making good use of the support rails placed there. The hot shower felt soothing as it forced the water through her hair, across her back and down her body. She quickly shampooed and rinsed her hair and then gave her lower legs and underarms a quick once over with the pink disposable razor.

Exiting the shower, Glenda nearly lost her balance due to the weakness in her left leg, but managed to recover her stumble, remarking, "Glenda, you're such a klutz!"

Wrapping a white fluffy towel under her arms and around her body, she tossed her damp hair back and looked in the vanity mirror. Red ringlets framed her face and her green eyes stared blankly back at her. There didn't seem to be much life in those eyes and her face was lacking that glow of happiness that was evident on the faces of others she observed.

"Glenda girl," she said, checking out her image in the mirror, "You need to make some changes...bring a little more light to your life."

She dropped the towel and turned, checking out her body in the long mirror on the door. Other than the long and predominant scar, which ran down the side of her left leg, her body was in pretty good shape. She had light porcelain skin and random freckles wherever the sun had touched it. Her breasts were full and firm and her hips round and soft, creating a shapely figure. Not that anyone would notice under her t-shirts and jeans.

Removing the tube of lotion from her black carry-on bag, she smoothed its contents lavishly over her skin. She slipped on her bra and panties and she reached into the drawer pulling out a clean pair of jeans and a light pink t-shirt.

Fully dressed, she stepped back and looked once more in the mirror, "Girl, you can't go to a memorial service dressed like that! It's time to do a little shopping," she said as she quickly ran a brush through her curls, creating loose waves which cascaded across her shoulders.

It was still early morning and Glenda was quite certain the stores wouldn't be open yet. So, she decided to have a bowl of cereal and cup of hot tea while reading the *Briarwood Enterprise.*

"Well, it looks like Maxine's Boutique is having a sale. Maybe I can find something there that I can wear to Laura's memorial service," she said, making a note of the store address. Turning back to the obituary page to once again check the time for the memorial, she commented, "Hmmmm....Well, Maxine's opens in about an hour, so that gives me some time to drive around town and get familiar with things. Maybe I'll be able to locate Maple Street. I should have enough time to get something to wear, come back here, change and still get to Laura's memorial. Oh, I need to remember to get a card, too...and maybe some flowers."

170

******

Mark woke to the sound of his clock radio broadcasting the local Briarwood news. He slowly sat up, ran his fingers through his hair and quickly pulled the covers over his bed (A habit created by his mother. He could hear her voice saying, *"Always make your bed as soon as you get up!"*) The D.J. was announcing the Obituaries and Mark heard that someone from the Briarwood Hills Nursing Home had died. Her memorial service was scheduled for that morning.   "I wonder if she was one of Mom's friends," he said, sipping his morning coffee. He still had one more day off work and hoped it would be the best day of his life, but he also promised to go see Betty Ann.   It wasn't that going to see his mother would make his day less wonderful, but who he really wanted to see was Glenda. Reasoning his mother might really need him this morning, especially if the woman who died was someone she knew personally, he added, "I'll go see Mom this morning and then...maybe...later...somehow...Glenda and I will meet."

******

"Good morning, Betty Ann," the nurse aide said as she knocked lightly on the door frame leading to Betty Ann's room. "Would you like some assistance this morning?"

Betty Ann was already up. She had self-transferred from her bed to the wheelchair and was in the bathroom. "I'm in h-here, d-dear," she called from behind the closed

171

door, "Decided t-t-to g-get myself r-ready th-this m-m-m-morning."

"Are you managing okay?" the nurse aide asked, listening outside the door.

"Y-yes, d-dear. I'm f-fine. Thank y-you. I'll c-c-call you if I n-n-n-need y-you." Betty Ann replied, knowing the sooner she could prove her ability to care for her personal needs the sooner she would be allowed to go back home. It was exhausting, but she did each movement slowly and with full concentration. Her legs were still very weak, but able to support her body for brief stands and transfers to and from the wheel chair. "M-Mark will b-b-be so s-s-surprised," she said, slowly brushing her soft white hair.

"Anybody home?" Mark's voice called out as he knocked softly on the bathroom door, "How about some breakfast?"

Betty Ann smiled at her reflection in the mirror. Even her smile was returning. There was hardly a trace of the paralyzing stroke she so recently experienced. Even the doctors were amazed.

When she opened the door, Mark was surprised to see his mother caring for her needs without assistance. "Mother...you look beautiful. Did you get yourself ready this morning?" he asked, bending down and gently kissing her cheek.

"Y-yes...yes...I d-did," Betty Ann replied with a grin, "I am g-getting m-m-much b-better."

"I can see that," Mark said, guiding his mother's wheel chair out of the room.

"N-No, M-M-Mark..." Betty Ann scolded, "I w-w-want to d-do it m-myself. I n-n-need to d-d- it m-myself."

"Oh...okay, Mom," Mark said, stepping back from the chair. Taking position along side of his mother, they slowly proceeded down the hallway to the dining room.

"Betty Ann paused and looked up at her son, "D-Did y-you h-h-hear about our l-loss h-h-here?"

"Yes, Mom," Mark responded bending down and gently taking his mother's hand in his, "Was she a friend of yours?"

"H-her n-n-name was L-Laura. Y-Yes, she w-w-was m-my f-f-friend," Betty Ann gently squeezed her son's hand and then continued rolling her chair forward, "Her m-m-memorial is t-t-today. I w-w-want t-t-to go. W-will y-y-you t-t-take me, please?"

Mark could tell it was important for his mother to attend her friend's memorial, but the thought of missing another chance to meet with Glenda also flashed in his mind. His mother and father had always taught him to give freely and to be the kind of person who helps others in need. His mother needed him...he would help.

"Yes...of course, Mom. I'll take you," he replied positioning her chair at their table, "We'll go together."

"Th-thank you, s-s-son," Betty Ann said, smiling, "It is s-s-so g-good to h-have y-you h-home" Reaching across the table, she placed her small aged hand over his, saying, "God B-Bless y-you, M-Mark. You are s-such a g-good son."

******

Glenda stepped into the office at the Bee-line Motel. There was a new assortment of brass bells hanging on the door knob that jingled as the door closed behind her. "I don't remember those being there before," she said quietly.

"That's because they weren't there before," Nellie said as she approached the desk from a side doorway

173

carrying a large calico cat. "Hello Miss Ashbury. Did you have a good night's rest?"

"Oh, yes...yes. It was wonderful," Glenda responded. There was a lump in her throat as her eyes were met by the big yellow eyes peering through the patches of black, orange and white fur.

"You like cats?" Nellie asked, noticing the strong focus Glenda had on the large ball of fur which was now purring in her arms.

Looking up there were tears in her eyes and she responded, "Yes...yes I did...I mean...I do."

"You okay, Hon?" Nellie asked, setting the large cat down, "You seem a little upset."

The big cat came out from behind the counter and gently leaned against Glenda's leg; purring and rubbing against this new human. Glenda bent down slowly and ran her fingers gently across the cats back as it arched itself against her hand. "She's beautiful," Glenda said, "It looks like someone dribbled paint across her back. What's her name?"

"I call her Sprinkles...just for that reason. When she was a kitten, I thought it looked like she got sprinkled with colored frosting...like a Halloween cupcake!" the woman laughed as the large cat rolled over on its back; hoping Glenda would rub her belly.

Glenda stroked the cat's fur along her tummy, and noticed the predominant nipples surrounded by matted, damp fur. "Looks like someone's got baby kitties somewhere," she said, smiling.

"Oh, yeah...she surprised us with a litter in my closet," Nellie said with a laugh, "We have five adorable little fur balls now that are ready to wean. One of them looks just like the momma."

"Lucky kitty," Glenda said softly, "Her momma is very beautiful."

"Say....you wouldn't be wantin' a baby kitten now..." Nellie said with a grin.

Glenda stood up and smiled, saying, "Oh...I don't know. I just lost my cat recently...I'm not so sure I'm ready for another one just yet."

But Nellie could see the longing in Glenda's eyes and said, "You know, there's always room for more love...don't ever forget that. When you're ready to see the kittens...just let me know."

"Okay...thanks," Glenda responded, "I appreciate that. Oh...I almost forgot why I stopped in. Can you tell me where Maple Street is?"

"Sure, Hon...Remember how you got to Stewart's Market?" Glenda nodded and Nellie continued, "Well, just go one more block and turn left. Then two more blocks and you'll see Maple Street. Is there someone you are looking for in particular?"

But once again Glenda decided she wasn't ready to share her information about the scrapbook with Nellie and replied, "I'll let you know...thank you, Nellie."

Glenda approached the turn, just past Stewart's Market, and took a deep breath praying softly, "Lord, help me know which way to go when I get to Maple Street...and if I find Betty Ann's house, please, please, dear Lord, help me find her."

Turning left she continued two more blocks to Maple Street, stopping at he intersection and carefully opening the scrapbook to one of the pictures of the house Betty Ann grew up in. She looked to the left and then to the right and her heart told her to turn left. About half-way up the street she saw it; the little tan house. It looked just like the one in the old photo. Instantly her thoughts went back to the stories in the scrapbook and the little house.

Glenda parked her car at the curb and turned off the motor. With both hands gripping the steering wheel, she glanced up at the cute little house. Growing on the trellis

175

was the winding pink rose bush. It felt strangely like home. Taking another deep breath and picking up the scrapbook from the seat beside her, she said, "Let's see if we can find your family."

Glenda carefully climbed the few steps leading to the front porch and recalled a picture in the scrapbook of Betty Ann and her dog sitting on the steps. There was a brightly colored mat at the door way which read, WELCOME FRIENDS and showed very little sign of wear.

Glenda knocked gently on the wooden screen door and waited. There was no response. She knocked again; this time with a little more force. But still there was no response. Gazing around the yard from the front porch, she could tell the house was well cared for. The yard was mowed and the flowers maintained.

"Maybe she's just at an appointment and will return later," Glenda reasoned, "Or perhaps she is out of town." Something in her heart assured her the little house was still Betty Ann's home. She looked at her watch, realizing she needed to get to the store if she wanted to find something to wear to the memorial service for Laura. Returning to her car she headed back toward down town Briarwood, and Maxine's Boutique; vowing to revisit the house on Maple Street later.

At Maxine's Glenda was able to find a long skirt with a soft floral print, a soft pink short- sleeved, light-weight cotton sweater and pale pink comfy leather pumps. Maxine, herself, assisted Glenda with her choices and said the soft pink looked wonderful with Glenda's red hair and skin tone. Glenda took her word for it. She also purchased a large green canvas bag.

Thanking Maxine, Glenda left and went to the store next door; the Briarwood Floral and Gift Shop where she purchased a sympathy card and found a statue of an angel holding a star. It reminded her of the falling star Betty Ann had referred to in the scrapbook. The shop owner promised to have them delivered to Petersen Funeral Home before the service started.

Glenda returned quickly to her room at the motel and changed into her new clothes. Turning slowly, she took pleasure in way the soft skirt flowed and gracefully hid the ugly scar on her leg. It was time to head to Laura's memorial, so she hung the canvas bag and its contents over her shoulder and headed out the door.

20.

Glenda arrived early at Petersen Funeral Home and was greeted by a woman dressed in a dark gray suit with a crisp ivory blouse. She assisted Glenda as she entered the parlor and directed her to the guest book. Glenda signed her name and address and removed a twenty dollar bill from her wallet in the canvas bag. She put it in a memorial envelope and slipped into a slot in the small wooden box marked, MEMORIALS FOR THE FAMILY. Looking around the chapel, she noticed the couple who shared the flight with her from Denver to Omaha seated in the pew on the right side of the aisle.

Front and center of the chapel was an open casket with light blue satin exposed and a spray of pink roses with baby's breath adorning the closed end. There was a white satin ribbon flowing from the flowers which read, MOTHER. On each side of the casket were stands with flowers and plants and the little angel that Glenda had purchased.

Glenda stepped closer and noticed the brown, gently positioned hands against the dark navy dress. Her eyes moved slowly toward the head of the casket focusing on the so still face of Laura Gibbons, with her salt and pepper hair neatly styled and her softly painted pink lips. Glenda gazed down at the still, lifeless figure in front of her and recognized the resemblance of the young woman she met on the plane in the old woman's face.

Glenda was suddenly startled by the gentle touch of someone's hand on the back of her arm. Turning, her eyes were met by the familiar eyes of the woman who sat by her on the plane. She smiled that same weary smile and said, "Thank you for coming."

Impulsively, Glenda embraced the woman and whispered, "I'm so sorry for your loss. She looks very peaceful." As the two women stood facing the casket, Glenda added, "You share many of her features."

The woman smiled and replied, "That's what Nick, my husband, says." Turning to Glenda she reached out her right hand saying, "By the way...my name is Tara Wilson. I guess we never really introduced ourselves;"

Glenda shook her hand gently, and said, "I'm Glenda...Glenda Ashbury. It's good to know you."

"Come, sit with us, Glenda. There's no reason for you to sit alone. There won't be anyone else coming except maybe a few from the nursing home," Tara held Glenda's hand firmly in hers.

Glenda could sense the longing for friendship in Tara's hazel eyes and softly said, "Sure...I'd be honored to sit with you." She took her place in the pew sitting to the left of Tara while Nick sat to Tara's right. It was the same way they had sat while on the flight from Denver to Omaha.

✳✳✳✳✳✳

Mark pulled into the handicapped parking place at Petersen Funeral Home. He lifted the wheel chair from the trunk and assisted his mother as she transferred from the car to her chair.

"Th-thank you M-Mark," Betty Ann said softly, smoothing the skirt of her pale pink suit. Pink was one of her favorite colors because Tim always told her it looked so good with her red hair. Of course her hair was white now, but seeing the pink brought back that good memory.

"You look beautiful today, Mother," Mark said, bending down to gently kiss her soft cheek.

179

"Th-that's s-s-sweet, d-dear. You l-l-look hands-s-some, t-too," Betty Ann replied.

Mark did look handsome in his khaki slacks, navy sport coat, cream dress shirt and geometric print necktie. He wasn't a dress suit sort of guy and was much more comfortable in jeans and a casual shirt, but knew his mother would expect him to dress respectfully for the service. He was glad that the slacks and sport jacket met with her approval. "Thanks, Mom," he whispered, while signing their names in the guest book. Then they entered the chapel.

Mark and Betty Ann sat toward the back as there was a shorter pew allowing space for her wheel chair. Scattered among the other pews were several others that they recognized from the nursing home, including Miss Swanson, the activities director, and several nurse aides who assisted in Laura's care.

Mark scanned the chapel and noticed the dark skinned couple at the front and assumed they were Laura's family, but wondered how the woman with red hair sitting with them was related. The sight of her soft red hair as it gently waved across the back of her pink sweater reminded him of Glenda and he felt the longing and anticipation once again to see her and talk to her.

The memorial was brief with the chaplain from the nursing home saying just a few words of sympathy to the family and reading several scriptural passages. Miss Swanson spoke of Laura fondly and recalled several humorous moments she shared with her during activities at the nursing home. She stated that Laura had a kind heart and a deep faith in God which manifested itself in everything she did. Then she addressed the family and stated how she wished they could have had the opportunity to know Laura, but that someday they would all meet again...in heaven. A tape recording of "Amazing Grace"

180

played softly throughout the chapel and the service was over.

"I w-w-want to g-give my respects to the f-f-family," Betty Ann whispered to Mark as she maneuvered her wheel chair away from the pew and into the aisle.

"Of course, Mom. I'll walk up with you," Mark said, stepping behind the chair then asking, "Do you want me to help you?"

"N-No...n-no, D-Dear. I w-w-want to d-do it m-myself," she whispered.

Approaching the front of the chapel, Mark's attention was on his mother, making certain she could handle the effort of rolling her chair the full length of the aisle. The couple, at the front, was accepting condolences from the few who attended Laura's service.

When Betty Ann reached the front, she wheeled her chair close to Laura's casket and tenderly peered over the side at her friend, lying so still among the shiny light blue satin. "Good-bye, dear Laura. May God and his angels welcome you to heaven. I will see you soon, my friend," she thought silently. Mark gently placed his hand on his mother's shoulder as she reached up and patted it affectionately. There was nothing he could, or needed, to say.

"Hello, Betty Ann," Miss Swanson said as she approached them, "I'm glad you were able to come today, too, Mr. Bryant. It's good to have you home from your trip." She reached out and gently shook Mark's hand, adding, "Please come with me. I want to introduce you both to someone very special." The three of them continued toward the couple...Laura's family.

Glenda was seated in the pew and partially hidden by Tara and Nick as they stood and spoke with the guests.

Miss Swanson approached Tara, saying, "Tara, this is the woman I spoke to you about...the one who did the painting for your mother."

Tara smiled softly at Betty Ann and gently took her hand saying, "Thank you so much for doing that. I guess she always wanted to go to California because that is where she heard I had gone. You made her very happy."

Betty Ann squeezed Tara's hand and said, "N-No, D-Dear...s-she m-made us all v-very h-h-happy. I'm B-B-Betty Ann. It is s-s-so n-nice to m-m-meet you."

Glenda leaned forward when she heard the woman say *THAT* name...the name of the woman she was seeking! She saw a lovely woman in a pale pink suit, holding Tara's hand and smiling. There was something very familiar about that smile. The woman glanced at Glenda, who was now peeking around Nick, and her blue eyes met Glenda's green eyes. Glenda felt an instant connection...an unexplainable bond.

Glenda raised her eyes to look up just as Mark bent down to see who his mother was smiling at. Their eyes met. Glenda slowly rose from the pew. Nick offered his assistance to help her stand and Glenda accepted it willingly. Her heart was beating wildly and she suddenly felt very weak.

"Excuse me," Mark said as he walked around his mother's chair and past Tara and Nick. When he reached Glenda, he took her hand in his and looking into her eyes said softly, "Don't you think it's time we talked?"

Glenda smiled up at Mark, tears streaming down her cheeks, and replied, "I have so much to tell you...where do we begin?"

Betty Ann wheeled her chair next to her son and the pretty red-head saying, "Let's s-start w-w-with in-tro-duc-tions. My n-n-name is B-B-Betty Ann..."

But before she could say another word, Glenda leaned toward her; taking her hand and softly saying, "I know. I've been searching for you, Betty Ann."

Betty Ann looked puzzled and glanced at Mark who appeared just as puzzled. Tara gasped and placed her hand

182

over her mouth as Glenda reached down to the pew and lifted the green canvas bag, handing it to Betty Ann.

"W-W-What's th-this?" Betty Ann asked softly.

"I believe there is something inside that belongs to you," Glenda said, smiling.

Betty Ann slowly opened the bag and carefully removed the old, tan, leather scrapbook. Her eyes filled with tears as she looked up at Glenda and stammered, "W-W-Where....h-h-how d-d-did you...."

Glenda smiled and repeated, "I have so much to tell you...where do we begin?"

******

The Nebraska sky glowed with another glorious mid-summer sunset. Glenda realized she now understood what Nellie, at the Bee-Line Motel, meant when she had told her there's always room for more love. Sitting with Mark on the steps of the little tan house on Maple Street, they watched as a little red headed girl playfully attempted to stuff a big calico cat into her doll stroller. The cat meowed slowly as if pleading to be rescued.

"Put Lucky Kitty down, Sweetheart. She doesn't want to ride in your stroller right now," Glenda said softly to her precious daughter. The little girl giggled and released the cat from her grasp then ran around the side of the house to the rose trellis, which she promptly started to climb.

Around the corner of the house, an old woman sat on a stone bench admiring the beauty of the sunset while observing the antics of her granddaughter. It was good to be home again. And so good to have the house full of family and laughter once more. Often she could see herself in the behavior of the little red headed girl as she played around the yard...and this was just one of those moments.

"You get down from that trellis, Mary Rose!" the old woman called, laughing, from the garden. "Don't you know if you break the trellis the roses will have nowhere to climb? You don't want the roses to lose their way do you?"

The little girl jumped down from the trellis and picked a pink rose from the vine. Handing the rose to her grandmother, she innocently asked, "Nana, where would the roses go if they lose their way?"

Betty Ann thought for a moment. Taking the little girl's hand, she smiled and replied, "Let's go ask your mother."